Also in Alex Morgan's The Kicks series

SABOTAGE SEASON

WIN OR LOSE

ALEX MORGAN

Simon & Schuster Books for Young Readers
New York   London   Toronto   Sydney   New Delhi

SIMON & SCHUSTER BOOKS FOR YOUNG READERS
An imprint of Simon & Schuster Children's Publishing Division
1230 Avenue of the Americas, New York, New York 10020
This book is a work of fiction. Any references to historical events, real people, or real places are used fictitiously. Other names, characters, places, and events are products of the author's imagination, and any resemblance to actual events or places or persons, living or dead, is entirely coincidental.
Text copyright © 2013 by Alex Morgan and Full Fathom Five
Cover illustration copyright © 2013 by Paula Franco
All rights reserved, including the right of reproduction in whole or in part in any form.
SIMON & SCHUSTER BOOKS FOR YOUNG READERS is a trademark of Simon & Schuster, Inc.
For information about special discounts for bulk purchases, please contact Simon & Schuster Special Sales at 1-866-506-1949 or business@simonandschuster.com.
The Simon & Schuster Speakers Bureau can bring authors to your live event. For more information or to book an event, contact the Simon & Schuster Speakers Bureau at 1-866-248-3049 or visit our website at www.simonspeakers.com.
Also available in a Simon & Schuster Books for Young Readers hardcover edition
Book design by Krista Vossen
The text for this book is set in Berling.
Manufactured in the United States of America / 0214 OFF
First Simon & Schuster Books for Young Readers paperback edition March 2014
2 4 6 8 10 9 7 5 3 1
The Library of Congress has cataloged the hardcover edition as follows:
Morgan, Alex (Alexandra Patricia), 1989–
Saving the team / Alex Morgan. — First edition.   pages cm. — (The Kicks ; [1])
Summary: After moving to California, seventh-grader Devin is afraid she will not make the soccer team but finds, instead, a team so bad that she is compelled to take the lead and turn it into something the players and coach can all be proud of.
ISBN 978-1-4424-8570-9 (hardback) — ISBN 978-1-4424-8571-6 (pbk)
[1. Soccer—Fiction. 2. Leadership—Fiction. 3. Friendship—Fiction. 4. Moving, Household—Fiction. 5. Family life—California—Fiction. 6. California—Fiction.] I. Title.
PZ7.M818Sav 2013   [Fic]—dc23   2013002033
ISBN 978-1-4424-8572-3 (eBook)

full fathom five

FOR MY MOM AND DAD,

WHO HAVE SACRIFICED AN INCREDIBLE AMOUNT

SO I CAN FOLLOW MY DREAM

CHAPTER ONE

I was running as fast as I could, moving so quickly, the other players were a blur. My best friend, Kara, was streaking up the field not far behind me, the two of us connected by an invisible string. After dribbling around a defender, Kara lofted the ball way up high, incredibly high, a pass meant for one special person.

As the sold-out crowd rose to their feet, chanting my name, I leaped into the air. "Dev-in! Dev-in!" They knew what was coming.

Soaring over the other team's defenders, I closed my eyes as I flicked my head forward, aiming directly for the center of the ball. I headed it in, right past the goalie's outstretched hands. *Goooooal!* My teammates were already racing over to congratulate me. They lifted me off the ground and bounced me up and down on their shoulders.

"Devin, Devin, wake up!"

My eyes popped open, focusing on my little sister, Maisie, who was jumping up and down on my bed.

Ugh, I was so not ready to wake up yet.

"First day of school!" she shouted. "Dad's gonna drive!" I tried to throw my pillow at her as she bounced out of my room, but it barely cleared the edge of the bed. I was exhausted.

I leaned back and sunk into my familiar mattress, wishing it would suck me in and transport me back home. I could be in Connecticut right now, getting ready to conquer the seventh grade as half of Kara-and-Devin. (I was okay with Kara's name being first because she was five weeks older.)

This was supposed to be the year my best friend, Kara, and I became seventh-grade co-captains of the Milford Middle School Cosmos and got to wear the yellow captain armbands with the big letter C on them. Instead that C now stood for "California," where my family had moved to.

Seeing dream Kara made me miss real-life Kara, so I did what I do whenever I feel that way—I reached for my phone in the hopes of having a message from her. The only thing I asked my parents for when we moved was unlimited texts so I could be in touch with Kara constantly.

Mom says it's 2 early to ring u. Striped polo, red skirt. Sent a pic. Bye!

I clicked open the picture Kara had texted me. In it Kara was holding the camera in front of her full-length mirror, capturing a shot of her wearing the outfit she'd described. Her long, brown hair was swept into a high ponytail. She had a huge grin on her face, and her big blue eyes had that mischievous look they always did. I let out a big sigh. I missed her.

Kara and I had agreed that we'd still pick out our school outfits together, like we always used to do, but with the three-hour time difference, we couldn't exactly call each other up in the mornings. I may have just woken up, but Kara had already been at school for two hours by now. I would have to figure out what to wear without Kara's help. Not that I couldn't dress myself or anything. It was just a fun thing we'd done each morning. But everything was different now.

"Devin!" Mom's voice called from downstairs. "You'd better be getting dressed. We have to get to school early and get your enrollment paperwork done."

"Okay, okay, I'm coming," I groaned. I had been awake for only five minutes—and I wasn't exactly ready to go rushing off into my new life.

"Setting a course for Kentville Middle School," Dad said as he pretended to push buttons on the console of our family car. He even made the accompanying beeping sounds as he prepared to pull out of the garage.

"Whoosh!" Maisie cried, throwing her head back as Dad pushed the car up to a whopping forty miles an hour. Maisie was eight and didn't mind playing along with my dad's silly games. I, on the other hand, was far too nervous to even pretend to want to join in.

Meanwhile my mom turned around and handed me and Maisie each a bottle of water.

"I already packed water in your backpacks," she said. "But take extra. It's important to keep hydrated!"

Maisie and I exchanged eye rolls. If we had a dollar for every time our mom told us to keep hydrated, we'd be rich. It was like she thought we were going to dry up or something. And now that we had moved to California, which is warmer all year than Connecticut, she had really gone water crazy, offering us a glass every time we turned around. But that's Mom. She's a big health-food nut too, so I'd rather have the water than her famous green smoothie. Blech.

"Can't I have fruit punch?" Maisie pleaded. Mom shook her head. It was an argument they had all the time. What Mom didn't know was that Maisie traded her snacks for fruit juice. I hoped she'd find some kids at her new school who liked kale chips; otherwise she'd be out of luck.

I squeezed my eyes shut so I couldn't see us driving closer and closer to school. The drive might feel longer that way, I hoped. Sensing my nerves, my mom reached back from the front seat and gave my hand a squeeze. I opened my eyes briefly to give her a small smile, and then closed them again.

The problem was, I was completely unprepared for a new school. Mom had given me a "Welcome to Kentville

Middle School" packet—but that hadn't told me anything I really wanted to know. Like, for example, who would talk to me? That was not adequately covered. Where did the nice, normal seventh graders eat lunch, and would it be awkward if I sat with them? There was not one hint or spot marked out for me on the brochure's map. How would I fit in with the kids from Kentville? The pamphlet was useless there, too.

The only thing that gave me a glimmer of hope was the fall calendar tucked into the brochure. Soccer try-outs were being held today—the first day of school! I might not know if I'd fit in with the Kentville kids, but one thing I did know for sure was that I was pretty good at soccer. But that had been back in Connecticut. Half the US women's soccer team came from California. What if all the kids were superhuman soccer-playing robots? At the very least, competition for spots on the team would be fierce. But just the thought of playing soccer again made me happy, *if* I could make the team. It would be nice to play soccer in real life again, not just in my dreams. I hoped I didn't get totally creamed at the tryouts.

Soccer or not, I still didn't have the answer to the biggest question of all: How would I survive without Kara?

The one summer we'd spent apart, when Kara had gotten sick and couldn't leave for sleepaway camp with me, I hadn't managed to meet any new friends until she'd showed up three weeks later. It was the worst. What if I didn't meet anyone here, either? Who would come save me now?

Lost in thought, and with my eyes still screwed shut, I didn't notice we'd arrived at my new school until Dad pulled up right in front of the entrance, and jerked the car to a stop. "Here we are at our first destination," he announced. "Please disembark to the right."

Kentville Middle School was a huge, plain-looking brown-and-yellow stucco building. It looked just like a normal school—not the glamorous California school I'd built up in my head. In front of the building was a big green gate, with the door swung wide open.

Students poured in through the gate, a sea of unfamiliar faces. A clump of kids was hanging out by the flagpole in front, with the US and California flags fluttering in the slight morning breeze.

Mom got out of the passenger seat, her papers scattering to the ground. "Devin, let's go," she said, scrambling to pick everything up. I ran my hands through my long, stick-straight brown hair to make sure it was presentable before opening the door and stepping outside into the warm, dry California air.

I took a deep breath. *Kentville Middle School, here I come.*

"Devin Burke?" my math teacher, Mrs. Johnson, called out.

"Here," I said.

I was in my first period—algebra class. Algebra was usually just for eighth graders, but I had always been good at math, and my placement test had landed me here.

"Ah," Mrs. Johnson said, "I see you're our only seventh grader this year. And you're new to Kentville, I take it?"

"Yeah," I said. "I moved here from Connecticut."

"Well, welcome to the West Coast!" said Mrs. Johnson. "Our class is delighted to have you."

But they didn't exactly look delighted. They weren't paying attention to me at all, as a matter of fact. I guess that's what it was like to be the only seventh grader in a classroom full of eighth graders.

But even in my homeroom of seventh graders, it had been clear that most people already had their friends and weren't necessarily on the market for a new one. I understood that. In Connecticut, because I'd had Kara, I hadn't really tried to meet new people. I hadn't been unfriendly or anything, but making new friends hadn't been a priority. I was sure it was the same way for people here. I was afraid making new friends was going to be impossible. It wasn't going to happen in algebra class, that was for sure. Here's who talks to the only seventh grader in algebra: no one, apparently.

There was a group of girls in the back, who I kind of got a good glimpse of. One look and I could just tell they were the cool girls. They had their hair pulled up high in messy topknots, and their lips were shiny with gloss.

Looking at those girls, and the other girls in the class, one thing was immediately obvious: California girls dressed way differently from Connecticut girls. First of all almost every girl in class had flip-flops dangling from her feet. I looked down at my Converse sneakers. *I gotta ask Mom to get me some flip-flops.* Generally speaking, California style seemed way more easygoing than back East. I didn't see one polo shirt in the crowd. No plaid, either. Preppy was definitely not in here the way it always was in Connecticut. My carefully creased khakis were one of a kind here, and that paired with my crisply ironed dress shirt, I felt a little stiff. Luckily, long, flowing hair seemed to be the thing in California. At least I met that criteria.

"Devin, want to solve for x?" Mrs. Johnson said to me, breaking my concentration. On the board she had written down a too-easy equation.

As I got up to solve the problem, I thought, *Yeah,* x *is how many friends I've made so far. X equals none.*

At lunch I walked into the cafeteria, alone, and was completely overwhelmed. It seemed like everyone knew exactly where to sit, and they were already there, chatting away happily and eating their lunches. Not knowing what to do, and too scared to go sit with a total stranger, I brought my packed lunch to the steps by the library and pulled out my book to read so I didn't look like a complete loser.

After finishing my food, with plenty of time left in the lunch period, I didn't know what to do with myself. I snuck into a bathroom stall to call Kara. I knew we weren't allowed to use phones during school hours, but if I didn't talk to somebody soon, I was going to explode. A trio of girls came in to hang out and gab in front of the mirror, and after a few minutes of primping, it didn't seem like they were going to leave.

Not wanting to risk anyone overhearing my phone call, I settled on just texting Kara.

1st day is horrible. Haven't met anyone. =(

Her response came back right away. *Awww, it'll get better. Gina and Vida say hi!* Gina and Vida were two of our soccer friends. I immediately felt jealous that Kara was hanging out with them and not me.

Watr u doing?! I wrote.

School's out, going 2 mall. Go meet people! =P

It's SO not that easy! I responded. I wanted to tell her exactly what my morning had been like, but that would have to wait till later on Skype.

Just be urself, ur so outgoing! I didn't feel outgoing. I felt like a girl who was hiding out in a bathroom, crouched on a toilet seat. My phone buzzed again. *U R AWESOME!*

Thanks, call you later. Luv u!

The primping girls finally left the bathroom. I stuffed my phone into my bag and unlocked the bathroom stall. Having texted with Kara, I felt a bit better. A little more hopeful. Maybe Kara was right. Maybe if I was more my usual outgoing self, I'd be okay after all.

At least my next class was girls' PE. What a relief. I might have been having trouble meeting people, but sports I could do. I was especially relieved when I learned we'd be playing kickball. I loved kickball. I was psyched when it was finally my turn at the plate.

As the pitcher rolled the ball toward me, I dug in my back foot and then swung forward with my right. The rubber ball took off with a satisfying *thwok*, launching way out into the outfield. It was nice to see all those years of soccer come in handy. I rounded the bases, stopping only when I got to third.

"Woo-hoo! Great kick," the girl at third base said to me as I skidded to a stop. Her braided black hair was all bunched up into a messy ponytail. She had on a bright blue headband, and her wrists were filled with bracelets.

She snapped her gum as she talked. "Let's see you do it again next time," she said, punctuating her friendly challenge with a smile and a bubble burst. "I'm Jessi, by the way."

My next turn up I kicked the ball harder, aiming it at right field, toward a tall girl with thick black bangs that went straight across her forehead. She took a few long steps backward, holding her arms out to catch the ball, but then she tripped over her own feet and fell down, right on her backside. When I saw that, I knew I had some time, so I looked straight ahead and chugged for third base again.

"Emma, get up," Jessi called out to the struggling girl. "The ball is behind you!"

When I breezed by third on my way home, Jessi gave me a high five, even though she wasn't on my team. The girls on my team congratulated me when I got back to the dugout. It was the best part of my day so far, hands down.

Later, when we were headed back to the locker rooms to change, Jessi and Emma caught up to me.

"Hey, do you play soccer?" Jessi asked. "Because you have a mean right foot."

I smiled. "I do! Well, I did. Back home in Milford. And by the way, my name is Devin."

"Well, Devin, you have to come to soccer tryouts— they're right after school today," Emma said.

I nodded. "I know, but I'm a little nervous."

"Nervous?" Jessi asked in disbelief. "With that kick of yours?"

I sighed. "But California is famous for its soccer players. I'm guessing everyone on the team can kick like me or better."

Jessi and Emma looked at each other and burst out laughing. Jessi was doubled over with her eyes squeezed shut, and Emma covered her face with her hands as she laughed. I was totally confused. What was so funny?

"Oh, Devin," Jessi said as she recovered from her laughing fit. "I'm sorry to burst your bubble, but the Kentville Kangaroos stink!" Emma nodded in agreement, still grinning.

I couldn't believe what she was saying. "Really?" I asked, shocked. "Then why are you guys trying out?"

Jessi shrugged. "I love soccer. And it'll be fun, I guess. There's no pressure to win, that's for sure. And I heard we get out of class early for games and stuff. That's always a plus in my book."

Emma laughed and nudged Jessi with her elbow. "You'd do anything to get out of class. But seriously, Jessi is a great player." Jessi smiled modestly when Emma said that. "And I love to play too—even if I'm not always that, um, coordinated," Emma said, and they both giggled. "But I'm a huge soccer fan! And I heard that Coach Flores is really nice, but they say she's kind of flaky, too. This will be our first year on the Kentville team—it's only for seventh and eighth graders."

"The Kangaroos will have a better season this time around," Jessi said confidently. "Because we'll be on the team!

"They did win only one game last year," she added.

Emma giggled again, and said, "And wasn't that because the other team forfeited?"

Jessi nodded.

"Wow," I said, shaking my head. "I can't believe it. I thought everyone would be like Olympic soccer stars here." How could this be true? Maybe the Kangaroos weren't good by California standards, which were way high. The team was probably still awesome compared to my East Coast team. Or maybe Jessi and Emma were exaggerating about how bad the team was to make me feel less nervous about tryouts.

"You still have to try out," Jessi pleaded. "If we get more players like you, maybe it really will be a winning year for the Kicks."

"The Kicks?" Now I was totally confused. "I thought you were the Kangaroos?"

"It's a nickname for the girls' team," Jessi said.

Emma nodded. "It goes way, way back. We're not even sure where it came from. Maybe because, you know, kangaroos kick?" She shrugged.

"The Kicks," I said, smiling. "That's cute. But the team couldn't always have been horrible, to get a cool nickname like that?"

"Who knows?" Jessi sighed. "But it's a new season," she added hopefully, "and maybe you, me, and Emma will be the Kicks' new lucky charms! Here's hoping all three of us make the team. Honestly, Devin, I think you'll be a shoo-in."

"Maybe we'll even beat Pinewood," Emma added optimistically.

Jessi snorted. "Don't count on it. They're the best team in our league. I'd be happy to win *any* game!"

For a second I felt crushed hearing how bad the soccer team was, even though I still found it hard to believe. Then I flashed back to my desperate texts to Kara from the bathroom. She'd told me to be myself, and as soon as I had been, I'd met two nice girls who played soccer too! Terrible soccer team or not, things were starting to look up in the friend department. And if the other girls trying out for the team were this nice too, I definitely wouldn't be eating lunch on the library steps or hiding out in the bathroom anymore.

"Tryouts after school, got it," I said with a smile. If

it meant spending more time with Jessi and Emma, I'd squash my nerves and give it a go. "I'll see you there!"

"Excellent!" said Emma.

Now if only I could figure out where Mom had unpacked my soccer stuff . . .

CHAPTER TWO

My mom picked me up from school so I could go home and change before the tryouts. It was just us in the car. I breathed a sigh of relief that my dad wasn't there doing his corny sound effects, and that Maisie couldn't interrupt us, because I couldn't wait to tell Mom about my day.

"I want to hear everything!" Mom said as she navigated through the sea of cars and buses.

"First of all, I'm going to need flip-flops," I said, and then I filled her in on West Coast fashion, Jessi and Emma, and the news about how bad the soccer team was.

"It's a new year and a new team," Mom said to encourage me. "You never know how the season will go."

We pulled up in front of our new house. I raced out of the van. "I almost forgot," my mom called after me, "but Kara called. I told her you'd call her before tryouts. Oh, and make sure to grab some water to take with you!"

I couldn't wait to tell Kara how my day had turned around since we'd texted earlier. I ran into the house, dialing Kara on my cell phone as I headed upstairs to get my soccer stuff.

"Guess what?" I asked her when she picked up. "I met a couple of girls—Jessi and Emma—in my gym class today. We played kickball and they were really cool. And it turns out that Jessi is in my English class too." Jessi had shrieked and given me a high five when I'd walked into my last class of the day. It had felt great to see a familiar face in one of my classes for a change.

"Yes! See, I knew you'd make friends," said Kara.

"I hope we'll be friends," I said. "But I am so nervous about tryouts today. I hope I can make the cut in California. Even though Jessi and Emma told me I had nothing to worry about, I'm worried they were just trying to make me feel better."

"What do you mean?" Kara asked.

I quickly filled her in on the Kicks.

"Jessi and Emma could be exaggerating," Kara said. "But it doesn't matter where you play, Devin. California, Connecticut, or Brazil—you're a great player, and *where* you're playing can't change that!"

Kara always knew how to cheer me up. "You are *the best* best friend ever!" I told her.

"Don't forget your pink headband," Kara reminded me. Since everyone looks the same in soccer uniforms, Kara and I always used to wear bright pink headbands when we played so we'd stand out. Putting them on together had been our special pregame ritual.

Kara filled me in on her day before we got off the phone. Dad drove me back up to school.

"Kick some butt, Devin!" said my dad, giving me a hug of encouragement. My dad loved watching me play soccer. He'd be so happy if I made the team here. But I couldn't help feeling the butterflies fluttering in my stomach. Even with Kara's pep talk, and Emma and Jessi telling me not to worry, it was still hard to believe that I wouldn't be facing Olympic-athletes-in-the-making.

As I climbed out of the car, I saw a group of girls already on the field running laps, so I had to get my equipment on fast. As soon as I got to the field, I took off my shoes and socks, pulled my shin guards from my bag, and began to pull them onto my feet.

"Those are some seriously fun socks," Jessi said, complimenting the electric blue polka-dotted pair spilling out of my bag. Jessi had just arrived too, but she seemed to be in no rush, plopping down right next to me, as casual as can be. "Check these out," she said, tugging a pair of lime-green-and-white-striped socks out of her satchel.

"We should each trade a sock," she said, grinning. "Here, take this sock, and I'll take one of yours." Before I could respond, Jessi tossed me one of her socks and held out her hand for mine.

I grinned. "Cool!" I passed her one, and we each continued to get ready. As Jessi had her head down tying her cleats, a tall girl with dark hair walked by and gave us both a dirty look. It was so nasty, it could have scorched the grass under the bench we were sitting on. Before I could even say anything to Jessi about it, the girl walked away and Jessi, all laced up, jumped to her feet, not even noticing.

"Jessi," someone yelled from the bottom of the bleachers. "Let's go!"

"Gotta go." With that, Jessi leaped over the short railing and raced toward the field. I wasn't sure if I'd just cemented a new friendship or if I'd just given away a perfectly good sock. I hoped it was both.

Out on the field a short woman wearing a bright blue athletic hoodie and black soccer shorts blew a whistle. "Welcome, ladies! I'm Coach Flores. Who's ready to have some fun?" she asked enthusiastically, smiling from ear to ear. "One more lap, then line up at the eighteen and we'll get started."

Just one more lap? I scrambled to finish getting ready. My shoes finally on, I bolted off the bench, afraid I wasn't going to have time to warm up. I hurried to make a loop and then joined everyone else at the top of the penalty box.

"We're going to start with a quick scrimmage. Count off ones and twos. The twos go toward that goal," Coach explained. "And the ones stay here with me. Remember to relax and have fun!"

As the girls started counting off, my insides knotted

up. Easy for Coach Flores to say "relax." I hadn't touched a soccer ball since Connecticut, and I definitely wasn't ready for a game yet, even a practice game, especially with unfamiliar teammates. Even though Jessi and Emma had claimed the team stunk, I wanted to impress the coach. Why couldn't we do drills first? Drills were predictable. And they gave everyone a turn, which was fair for tryouts, unlike scrimmages, where someone would have to pass me the ball for me to show off my skills. What if nobody passed to the new girl at school?

Peering ahead, I tried to see if Jessi and Emma would be ones or twos. The girl directly to my right was really short, which made it easy to see over her head and spot Emma, who towered over the other girls. She was standing with Jessi, who waved when she saw me.

The tiny girl beside me was anxiously chewing on the ends of her bobbed strawberry-blond hair. At least I wasn't the only one who felt anxious. Seeing her made me feel even more nervous. If the team was as bad as Jessi and Emma said, why was this girl nervous too?

"What did I miss?" somebody said, sliding into line beside me. "I decided to run an extra lap. I wasn't warmed up enough."

"We're counting . . ." My voice trailed off. It was the girl who had given me and Jessi that nasty look. She towered over me, her dark hair neatly braided and crisscrossed over her head like a crown. She wore a shiny white jersey with matching white shorts.

"Um, we're counting off for a scrimmage," I repeated. This is what I imagined a California soccer player would look like. Perfect. Unbeatable. The butterflies in my stomach invited a few friends over and started dancing the cha-cha.

Too intimidated to look at her directly, I gazed down at the ground as I nervously fiddled with my pink headband. And that's when I saw them.

Her shoes. Pure white leather with electric blue accents and silver stripes down the side. They were so *fancy*. Nobody spent that much money on shoes unless they were really good, right? And since she was next to me in line, we were for sure playing against each other. Great. I tried to remind myself what Jessi and Emma had said about the team's record. They'd seemed to think I'd be a shoo-in. I needed to relax. I was on my way to totally psyching myself out.

"Coach Flores is such a joke. Why is she having us do a scrimmage?" the girl said. "We should just do drills. My dad said she should have been fired after last year's disaster of a season. I tried my best, but even I couldn't save this team. But this year is going to be different," she added, with a determined look on her face.

If she had been on the team the year before, that would make her an eighth grader. She was a little full of herself, and I breathed a sigh of relief she wasn't in my algebra class, but I had to admit that I did agree with her about the drills.

"Yeah, it is weird that we're not doing drills first," I said.

"Scrimmages are the worst for a tryout. It's so hard to be noticed when everyone's running around. But this team is so awful anyway, what does it matter?" She shrugged.

I didn't know what to say to that. I found myself staring at her shoes again. "Your shoes are really cool," I offered.

"Aren't they?" she asked. "My dad got them for me. 'Dress for the job you want, not the job you have,' he always says. It's what I wore for tryouts for the travel soccer team I'm on. It's a waaaayyyy better team than this group of losers. Some Pinewood girls are even on my travel team. They're the real deal."

Pinewood again, I thought. Jessi and Emma had said they were the best team in the league. I gulped. If she was playing with girls from that team, she had to be good.

She looked down at my legs and sneered. "Nice socks," she said sarcastically. "You know they don't match, right?"

My jaw dropped. I couldn't believe she was making fun of me. And I didn't even know her name! Before I could think of how to reply to that, she barreled on.

"You're new here? I saw you talking to Jessi."

"I-I'm Devin," I stammered, still at a loss as to how to deal with her rudeness.

"I'm Mirabelle," she said. "Good luck. You're going to need it, especially if you hang out with Jessi."

I had no clue why Mirabelle disliked Jessi so much. Being the new girl definitely had its disadvantages. The butterflies decided to hold a family reunion. I felt like I usually did after drinking one of my mom's green smoothies, and I tried to shake the queasy feeling. Mirabelle was intimidating. If I let her get to me, I could blow tryouts. I needed to stay focused. But Mirabelle's sneering smile kept floating through my mind.

After we finished counting off, Coach Flores waved us out onto the field. "Fantastic job, everyone!" she cheered. "Now just go on out there and have fun. Pick a position and make sure you've got someone on goal."

Just pick a position? That sounded like pure chaos to me. I played striker, so I rushed ahead to claim a spot at center field. But there were already a few girls arguing over who got to play striker. I'd never get a spot. So I rushed back to play midfield—my next-best position.

Jessi, who was a one like me, ran by me on her way to grab a spot, giving me a concerned look. "I'd stay away from Mirabelle if I were you. She's mean." She raced off before I could answer. I had been able to figure that one out on my own. I wondered once again what was going on between Jessi and Mirabelle, but before I could think about it any more, Coach Flores blew her whistle to start the scrimmage.

All at once, it seemed like, everyone started screaming.

"Get the ball!"

"I'm open!"

"Over here!" It was total madness on the field, just like I'd feared.

When a high looping ball finally came drifting over to me, a horde of charging maniacs pounced. Flustered, I booted the ball away. Half the girls watched as the ball sailed back over their heads. Then they turned to chase after it like a pack of golden retrievers.

Even though there was a soccer ball and a bunch of players on the field, this did not feel like soccer. Organized soccer, anyway.

"This is crazy," I said out loud, even though nobody was around me.

"I know, isn't it?" Surprised by the voice, I looked over, and there was our goalie, squatting comfortably nearby. She was way outside the penalty box area. The goalie's yellow gloves looked even brighter against her all-black outfit. Her eyelids had dramatic, thick black eyeliner swiped across them, curling up at the ends. It gave her a very fierce look when she squinted.

"Shouldn't you be back there?" I asked. She wasn't in position to stop anything where she was.

"You must be new. I'm Frida," she said. "And I'm trying to *not* make the team."

"Trying to not make the team?" I asked. "Then why are you here?"

"My mom," said Frida. "I'm in drama club, and she wants me to be more 'well-rounded,' whatever that means. Thinks it'll help me get into college. Heads up!"

Unexpectedly the short girl with the strawberry-blond hair, the one who had been nervously chewing the ends of her hair, emerged from the pack with the ball, nobody anywhere near her. She dribbled up just past the halfway line when she saw the goal was empty. "Shoot it!" someone screamed.

The girl, who had been lost in concentration, looked up like she was surprised that she wasn't all alone on the field. When she saw everyone's eyes on her, she grew flustered and stopped suddenly. The ball kept rolling as she stood like a statue, frozen in place.

"That's Zoe," Frida said to me, shrugging. "She gets really nervous if anyone is watching her."

I felt bad for Zoe, but I saw my chance and charged forward and stole the ball from her. I headed toward the middle of the field. Looking up, I saw Jessi streaking in from the left wing. Applying just the right amount of lob, I floated a pass toward her, right between two defenders.

"Jessi!" I yelled out. Since the eighth graders couldn't agree on who should play striker, Jessi went in and grabbed the spot while they were too busy arguing to notice. She caught the ball in stride and one-timed it right past the other side's goalie, completing a beautiful goal. *Score!* That had to have gotten Coach's attention. I looked up to make sure she had seen, but Coach had an arm around Zoe and was giving her a pep talk instead of watching the game.

Jessi ran all the way from across the field to toss her arms around me in a huge hug.

"Such a great pass!" she exclaimed. "Sock sisters for life!"

I giggled, but the smile was wiped off my face as Mirabelle brushed by us midcelebration, her lip curled up. "Oh, get over it. It's one goal."

Jessi gave Mirabelle a dirty look and then rolled her eyes at me. "I'm sure if she scores, it will be the biggest deal ever. So lame."

On the next kickoff I moved to get the ball so I could look for Jessi again. From out of nowhere Mirabelle, who was on the other team, flashed in to take the ball away from me. *That was lucky*, I thought. Mirabelle then floated a perfect pass of her own to another player, leading to a gorgeous goal. "Nice pass, Mirabelle," Coach said. Great, *now* Coach was watching.

And Mirabelle was *good*. Fully engaged now, she kept twirling right through the chaotic pile of girls, showing off tricky step-overs, behind-the-back dribbles, and fancy ball juggles.

"Someone stop her," I said, gasping for breath after Mirabelle scored.

Then I saw Coach Flores look at her stopwatch and reach for her whistle. Scrimmage was going to end! I had to do something drastic if I wanted to be remembered for anything at all.

If I could stop Mirabelle, I would give everyone something to remember. The next time Mirabelle hurtled toward me, I lunged at the ball.

Anticipating my move, Mirabelle countered with a full 360-degree spin. I lost my balance and sprawled out on the ground, getting a mouthful of grass as she flew past me. I got my head up in time to see Mirabelle finesse the ball into the top left corner of the goal.

Coach's whistle blew. "That's enough, girls," she said. "You were all wonderful! Remember, no matter how you performed today, at least you all gave it your best. That's what counts. Tryout results will be posted tomorrow. Nice work, everyone."

I dropped my head down, totally humiliated. Coach Flores had to be kidding. I'd totally blown it. As Frida stopped to help me up, Mirabelle pranced by and mimed holding a video camera in her hand.

"YouTubed," she teased.

Brushing myself off, I stared after her.

"Oh, ignore her," Frida said. "We all fall down every now and then."

"Especially me," Emma said with a sheepish smile. "Believe me, however bad your fall just looked, I've done worse."

I was so embarrassed, I couldn't look at anyone.

Just then Jessi came up with Zoe in tow. "If that had been me, I would have just tackled her," Jessi said.

"Well, nobody's going to want me on the team after that," I said, bummed.

"Sure they will. You were great," Jessi assured me. "Um, were you watching? We might have a few good players, but the tryouts were a mess. Total disaster! You at least had an assist today!"

"I guess," I said. How would I explain to Kara and my parents that I couldn't even make the world's worst soccer team? "I hope you're right."

CHAPTER THREE

The next day during lunch I met Jessi, Emma, and Zoe behind the library building in the courtyard.

"Thanks for inviting me to eat with you guys," I said. "Having lunch alone yesterday was not exactly my idea of a good time."

"Oh, sure!" Jessi said. "The more the merrier."

This was the first time I'd seen Jessi not in gym clothes or practice stuff. She was wearing a bright pink thermal top, with distressed jeans ripped open at the knees. I had dug through my closet the night before for a basic striped scoop neck, and had ditched the khakis for simple skinny jeans. Emma wore a basic hoodie and slouchy jeans on her tall frame, while petite Zoe wore a lilac lace dress and glasses with oversize frames. She looked very California chic, while Emma looked like she could have just rolled out of bed.

"The list from the soccer tryouts is going to be posted after lunch," Emma said excitedly. "I hope we all made it!"

"I doubt I did," Zoe said sadly, "not after the way I froze up. I hope you guys have fun on the team without me."

"What happened, Zoe?" I asked. "You looked like you really knew how to handle the ball. It was only when everyone started calling to you that you seemed to get nervous."

Zoe blushed. "I don't know. When Emma, Jessi, and I are kicking the ball around, just the three of us, I'm fine. It's only when I feel like everyone is watching me, I freeze up."

Emma put her arm around Zoe's shoulder and squeezed. "She's better than fine when it's just the three of us—she's awesome!"

I smiled, feeling glad I had met such a nice group of girls. Imagine if everyone in this school were like Mirabelle! I shuddered. I had to know what was going on with her and Jessi. "So . . . what's the deal with Mirabelle?" I said.

Emma and Zoe groaned. "The Mirabelle saga," Emma said dramatically. "It never ends."

Jessi got a sad look on her face. "This is going to be hard to believe, but Mirabelle and I used to be besties."

"No way!" I felt my eyes grow wide. Jessi and Mirabelle were so different! Plus, Mirabelle was an entire grade ahead.

"She wasn't always like this," Jessi explained. "We live

on the same block and are neighbors, so we basically grew up together. Our parents are good friends. We knew each other before we even went to elementary school. Believe it or not, since Mirabelle was older, she always looked out for me."

"That *is* hard to believe," I said, still surprised at her revelation. "Mirabelle seems to look out only for herself."

Jessi nodded. "Now she does. We played soccer together in elementary school. Right before sixth grade she joined a traveling soccer team."

"She mentioned that," I said.

Jessi snorted. "I bet she did. Once she joined the team, which has girls from schools all over the county, she made friends with some girls from Pinewood."

"It's a super-expensive private school," Zoe explained.

"Yeah, I keep hearing about how good they are at soccer," I said.

"Both the boys' and girls' teams," Jessi said, and nodded. "Anyway, Mirabelle really wanted to go there, but her parents couldn't afford it. When she started sixth grade at Kentville, she completely changed. New wardrobe. New attitude. She acted like she didn't even know who I was. We stopped hanging out. My mom said it was because we were at different schools, but something about her had changed.

"I was so nervous to go into the sixth grade, knowing Mirabelle wouldn't even talk to me," Jessi said, and she smiled at Emma and Zoe. "But, luckily, I met these two on the first day, and I wouldn't trade them for all the Mirabelles on the planet!"

I shuddered as the image of an army of snotty Mirabelles popped into my mind. "If Mirabelle ditched *you*, why is she so angry at you?"

Emma and Zoe giggled as Jessi sighed.

"At first I missed the old Mirabelle," Jessi admitted. "I was hurt and confused. I thought if I could just make her remember all the fun times we used to have, we could be friends again. So one day last year I put this picture of us together in elementary school in her backpack, thinking it would remind her of what good friends we used to be. But the picture fell out in the locker room at her travel team's practice. All the Pinewood girls saw it and gave her a hard time about it."

"Why?" I wondered. "What's the big deal of having a picture in your backpack?" I kept one of me and Kara in my bag.

Emma began to giggle again. "Let's just say that Mirabelle wasn't always the perfect, fashionable person you see today."

"She had an awkward phase," Jessi explained. "And maybe she used to dress a little dorky. I didn't care. She was my friend. But she thought I'd planted the pic in her backpack on purpose, to embarrass her in front of her new friends. And she's been mad at me ever since."

"It's been a whole year?" I asked. "Boy, she really holds a grudge."

Jessi nodded. "So, sorry, but if you're friends with me, Mirabelle won't be very nice to you."

Emma and Zoe laughed again. "Yeah, because she treats everyone else sooooooo nice, right?" Zoe said, and chortled.

Jessi laughed. "Well, she is friends with all the popular eighth-grade girls," she said. "I guess she figured they were the only kids in Kentville good enough for her."

"Sometimes I think the only reason they're friends with her is because they're afraid of her," Emma said. "She is really bossy."

"And pretty rude," I added.

At that moment Frida appeared from around the corner. "The list from tryouts is up!" she said. "Here's hoping I didn't make it!"

Jessi jumped up and grabbed my hand to help me. The five of us raced toward the back of the gym and the locker rooms. My heart pounded as we ran, which didn't help my increasing nervousness. Even though the team didn't have a great record and seemed pretty disorganized, I really wanted to make it. I loved playing soccer, and I'd play anywhere I got the chance. Plus, I really liked Jessi, Zoe, and Emma.

As we got down to the locker room, a few of the girls from tryouts were already there, taking turns looking at a list of names posted on the wall.

"Frida, you're on here!" someone cried out from the front.

Frida let out a disappointed sigh at the news. Clenching her fist, she shook it at the sky. "Curses!" she exclaimed.

Jessi patted her on the back. "Sorry, Frida. You should thank your mom for me, though. You're a great player, even if you don't want to be."

"This is just going to cut into my audition time!" Frida wailed as she turned around and left the locker room.

Just ahead of us Emma was craning her neck, trying to see if our names were on the list.

"Devin, your name's on the list," Emma said. "And there's Jessi, Zoe, and me, too. We all made it!"

Zoe had a look of complete shock on her face. Emma gave her a hug. "Awesome! We're all on the team together," Emma cheered.

"Wait a second." Jessi got up close to the list and squinted. "Every person who tried out made the team!"

I squeezed past Emma to take a look at the list with my own eyes. I scanned the page, and ten eighth graders and nine seventh graders had made the team.

"Nineteen girls tried out yesterday," I recalled. "And everyone made it? Wow, that's a big team."

In soccer only eleven players could be on the field at a time. Most teams had spots for three or four alternates, but the Kentville Kangaroos had eight. That was a lot.

Emma shrugged. "That's Coach Flores for you. She wants everyone to have a chance."

I felt silly for even being nervous about tryouts. I could have sat on the field, recited nursery rhymes, and still made the team. That fact took away my feeling of accomplishment. I never imagined soccer in California would be like this! On the bright side, I had three new soccer friends to hang out with. But then Mirabelle's face popped into my mind. How was I going to deal with her?

CHAPTER FOUR

After school the next day I realized I'd forgotten my gym clothes, so I had to go home to change for our first practice. I didn't want to be late, so I hustled over to the Kentville soccer field as fast as I could. I had on my pink headband and was ready to go. As I arrived, I saw a bunch of boys stretching and getting ready for *their* practice. All of them were laughing and joking with one another, completely oblivious to me, standing by the far goalpost. There wasn't a girl soccer player in sight. Had I gotten something mixed up? When was our practice? This *was* where we'd had tryouts the other day.

Setting my bag down, I pulled out my phone and pulled up the schedule Coach Flores had e-mailed out to us yesterday. Yes, it was right there: Wednesday, September 3, two forty-five p.m., girls' practice. So where was everybody?

"What're you doing here?" a voice said from behind me.

I jumped. A skinny boy with spiky black hair squinted hard at me. He looked familiar. I was pretty sure he was in my English class.

"I'm, um, on the soccer team."

His eyes widened in surprise. "The guys' soccer team?"

"No!" I shook my head quickly. "I'm on the girls' team. But nobody's here. We're supposed to have practice now."

"The girls don't practice here," he said, stating the obvious. Then he offered something useful. "They're across the street, at the community park."

"Steven!" shouted some boys from across the field. "Get over here. We have to start!"

"Sorry. Gotta go," Steven said, trotting off backward while pointing across the street. "You better run."

I picked up my duffel and sprinted across the street in the direction he'd pointed in. Peering through the trees bordering the park, I spotted the girls' soccer team in the distance, and jogged over to them.

I broke into a sprint again and ran up to Coach Flores, who was talking to some of the players.

"I'm so sorry. I went to the wrong place," I said, still panting.

"No problem! I'm glad you made it," she said with a smile.

My old coach back in Connecticut would have made me run laps for being late, but I didn't tell Coach Flores that.

"Get in line and get ready to have fun!" she said cheerily.

The team was in one long line, zigzagging through a series of cones, dribbling soccer balls. Dust swirled around everyone's feet. Instead of the lush, well-maintained grass of Kentville's soccer field, the community park's field was basically dirt with a few tufts of weeds.

I shuffled into line with Jessi, Emma, and Zoe. "Where were you?" Jessi asked.

"Back at the field outside school."

"Like we'd ever practice there," said Jessi. "That's reserved for the boys. We get to use it only for actual games."

"But we had tryouts there the other day," I countered.

"Yeah, on the first day of school," Jessi said. "The boys' coach didn't want to overwhelm his boys with tryouts on the first day, so we got sloppy seconds."

"I just found out from Coach that we get the field for a game or practice only if the boys are at an away game," Emma added. "It's so unfair, right, Zoe?"

Zoe nodded. "I heard the seventh graders last year complaining they were second fiddle to the boys' team," she said regretfully. "I can see what they meant." We all looked bummed out at the news.

A girl standing in line in front of us turned around. "If we win some games, maybe we'll get some more respect around here." She had long blond hair with bangs cut straight across her forehead.

"Hey, Brianna," Emma said. "I thought after tryouts you

said you weren't going to be able to play soccer."

"I am kind of booked up," Brianna admitted. "What with chess club, Model UN, and the upcoming science fair. And I've got to keep my GPA up—I've still got a perfect four-point-oh. But I figured I would try to add soccer into the mix. After all, healthy body, healthy mind." She tapped her forehead.

I laughed to myself. I had a feeling Brianna would love my mom's green smoothie, which Mom always called brain food. Maybe Brianna would trade Maisie some fruit punch for one! But I felt myself frowning as my mind went back to where the girls' team ranked.

"Let me get this straight," I interrupted them. "The girls' team never gets to practice on the actual field? How are we supposed to get familiar with it?" At Milford whoever had an upcoming game got priority. That wasn't the case here, I guessed.

"That's not all," Brianna said. She pointed to the end of our field.

Something was missing. "Where are the goals?" I wondered.

"I was wondering the same thing, so I asked Coach as soon as I got here. See those trash cans down there?" Emma said, indicating two big bright orange cans spaced a few yards apart. "Those are the goalposts."

"How do we know how high to kick the ball?" I asked. Without any crossbars it would be hard to know if a ball would count as a score.

"Coach said we just kick it, and if she calls it a goal, it's a goal," Emma said. A junky field, trash cans for goals, and a coach who acted more like a preschool teacher than a soccer coach. Were all of our practices going to be like this?

"What drill are we doing?" I asked.

"We're dribbling through the cones," Jessi said. I watched the few girls ahead of us go.

"Are we dribbling the cones any special way?" I asked.

"Not yet. Coach just said to go through them. Any way you want," she said. Back at Milford, each time through the cones we'd focus on something different. Maybe just left-foot touches, or keeping the ball close with short dribbles for extra control. Something to learn and get better at. Here nobody seemed to be concentrating very hard on what they were doing.

On my turn I raced in and out of the cones, double tapping the ball on each crossover.

"Nice! How did you do that?" exclaimed Emma from behind me. "Let me try." When she stood still, Emma looked as athletic as Mirabelle. They were about the same height and athletically built. It was when Emma moved that the resemblance crumbled. As Emma tried to do the double tap, she kicked the ball too far ahead each time, which meant she had to run to catch up to it, and she overshot the cones.

I felt my back stiffen as Mirabelle laughed from behind us. Jessi twirled around to face her. "You do it, then." That was absolutely the wrong thing to say. I had no doubt Mirabelle could double tap. Triple tap even. Of course, when Mirabelle's turn came, she whipped through the cones perfectly. "Beat that," she said, gloating.

Ignoring her, Jessi went through the cones pretty perfectly herself. But when she turned around to see Mirabelle's reaction, Mirabelle was ignoring her, talking to a group of eighth graders and laughing. "Figures she'd pretend she didn't see me," Jessi said with an eye roll.

After ten more minutes of us dribbling around the cones, Coach Flores got us started doing a passing drill. If you could call it that. In Milford we would have called it a warm up. The whole thing consisted of standing around with everyone in a big circle, with one ball being passed around. You had to call out the name of the player you were going to pass to before you kicked the ball. It was kind of a mega-yawner.

But with the Kangaroos it was also an exercise in patience. You would think that not knowing everybody's name yet would make the drill more difficult for me, but no, that was not the case. Someone would call out "Grace!" and the ball would go to Mirabelle. "Anna!" and Emma would get bonked in the face.

"Nobody really knows what they're doing, do they?" I asked Jessi.

She shrugged. "It *is* only the first practice. But Coach Flores doesn't seem to care a whole lot about teaching us skills, does she?"

I looked over at Coach Flores, who was smiling like we had all just won a game. I never thought I'd meet somebody who was *too* nice, but Coach Flores seemed to fit that description. She stopped smiling just long enough to blow her whistle. "It's five o'clock!" she said, grinning once again. "Gather round, everyone."

"I hope you all had fun today! And congratulations for making the team!" I did a mental eye roll. All you had to do to make the team was show up! "You are all officially Kicks!" Some of the girls cheered at the mention of the team's nickname. "No pressure, but I wanted you to know our first game is at the end of the week," Coach continued once we'd all formed a circle around her.

"Wait—*this* week?" Mirabelle asked.

"Yes, on Friday night," she said. "But don't worry, you girls are looking great."

"But the game wasn't even on our schedule," Mirabelle complained.

"Oh, it wasn't?" said Coach Flores, looking confused. "I'm sorry. That is completely my fault."

How could we possibly have our first game when we barely even knew one another's names? Coach's touchy-feely-everyone-have-fun-no-pressure style had left us completely disorganized.

"We'll be traveling to Victorton, so we need at least eleven of you to show up. Otherwise tell me in advance if we need to forfeit. I know Friday's the weekend. And since I left it off the schedule, I'll understand if you guys made other plans." I swear, if she weren't our coach, I would have thought Coach Flores was encouraging us to skip the game.

"But if you do want to play, you'll have to get your permission slips signed to ride the bus." A stack of permission slips was passed around. Another sunny smile lit up her face as she looked around the circle. "Anyone have any questions?"

Mirabelle raised her hand. "We don't even know who our captains are yet. Are we going to choose them before the game?"

"Hmmmmm." Coach looked thoughtful. "What if we had one captain for the eighth grade and another for seventh?" The eighth-grade girls huddled together, Mirabelle in the middle. A lot of loud, intense whispering could be heard. It sounded like they were arguing.

Finally a tall, thin girl wearing red-and-white-striped socks emerged from the huddle. She didn't look happy.

"The eighth graders want Mirabelle as captain," she said.

"Thanks, Grace." Coach smiled at her. "Mirabelle is our eighth-grade captain."

Grace frowned slightly. I had seen her at tryouts. She was quiet but a good player with natural athletic ability. I didn't even know her, but I found myself wishing she were the eighth-grade captain instead of Mirabelle. Let's face it. I'd want anybody to be captain over Mirabelle!

Mirabelle looked around at everyone with a smug smile on her face.

"Okay, Mirabelle. You're our first captain. Any other nominations?" Coach asked.

"I nominate Devin!" Jessi said loudly and with a defiant look at Mirabelle.

I could hardly believe my ears. "Wh-what, me?" I sputtered out in surprise. "But I'm brand-new at this school! I hardly know you guys. Shouldn't you be captain?" I asked Jessi. She was a great player.

Jessi shook her head. "You'll be great, Devin."

If I had been back home, I would have been happy to step up with Kara, but this wasn't Milford or the Cosmos. I was still just getting the lay of the land here. And it was way too soon for me to be telling girls I barely knew what to do.

Out of the corner of my eye, I saw Mirabelle studying me. "I'll second Devin," she said. "Devin for co-captain." She smiled sweetly.

My mouth dropped open. Why did Mirabelle want me to be captain with her? And why was she being so nice?

"Are we all in agreement?" Coach asked. Everyone nodded. "Okay, Devin and Mirabelle are our co-captains!"

I was officially a captain of the Kangaroos. I hardly knew how it had happened. Was Mirabelle setting me up? I had no idea. I guessed I'd find out soon enough.

CHAPTER FIVE

As it turned out, the girl Kangaroos weren't the only team with a game on Friday—the boys' team had a game as well, at home. And unlike our game, which not even we knew about until Wednesday, the boys' game was getting major hype. They even called a pep rally for Friday afternoon, to be held in the school gymnasium.

At our practice Thursday night Coach Flores had asked us to sit up front near the boys during the pep rally to support our fellow Kangaroo soccer players. But now that we were there, it seemed like we were only in the way.

"Girls, can you step aside a little bit? We need some room for the banner." Coach Valentine, the boys' coach, shooed the girls' soccer team away from our front-row seats to make room for a giant banner. It had been carefully hand-painted, with the words "Go, Kangaroos! We're #1!" done up in neat block letters. Each of the Os were even little soccer balls. The gymnasium was packed too. Soccer was obviously a really big deal here at Kentville.

I had gotten to know some of the other seventh-grade girls on the team after the last practice, and they were really nice. We all sat together in the front row, wearing our blue-and-white uniforms. All our jerseys were kind of old, and some of the numbers were faded. Coach Flores had to use masking tape to remake my number thirteen. Everyone thought thirteen was an unlucky number, but it had always been good luck for me, like my pink headband.

I was sitting with Jessi, Emma, and Zoe. Also near us were Frida, Brianna—the girl I had met on Wednesday—and Brianna's friends Anna and Sarah, also seventh graders. Mirabelle and her eighth-grade pals were on the other side of the row. Which was fine by me. They hadn't actually gone out of their way to be friendly with us—especially Mirabelle.

"What are we, chopped liver?" Anna, who had short, curly black hair and dark brown eyes, asked. "'Girls, can you step aside a little bit?'" she said in a dead-on imitation of Coach Valentine's nasal voice.

"If we want to get the red carpet rolled out for our team, we're going to have to win some games," Sarah told her. She wore her long brown hair in two French braids.

Emma nodded. "The boys were state champions last year," she said. "That's major."

Frida rolled her eyes. "Yes, they're very good at kicking a ball around a field of grass. Everybody bow down to them.

I'd like to see one of them learn a Shakespeare soliloquy."

"Or win first place at the science fair!" Brianna chimed in.

I glanced over at Jessi, who wasn't paying attention to the conversation at all. In fact, she was scribbling furiously in her notebook. I tapped her on the shoulder.

"What are you doing?" I asked.

Jessi frowned. "My math homework."

"Don't you have math class right after the pep rally?" I said.

She hung her head sheepishly. "Yep, that's why I'm hurrying. I meant to do it last night, but *The Real Teenagers of Beverly Hills* was on, and I got distracted."

Before I could kid Jessi about watching a silly reality TV show instead of doing her homework, Coach Valentine picked up the microphone and motioned for the band to begin. The drummers started a slow drumroll. "Attention, please!" he announced. "Will everybody please give a big hand to your championship Kangaroo boys' soccer team!"

As the crowd cheered, the team came crashing through the paper banner. They ran toward the front of the stage, throwing out handfuls of candy from their pockets. The auditorium roared. People actually leaped out of their seats, arms outstretched, trying to get more candy. It was insane.

"They better throw some candy over here," Jessi said, dropping her notebook to the floor. "I can't sit still for long without some sugar. Over here!" she shouted.

"And now," said Coach Valentine, "your boys' soccer

team seventh-grade captain, Cody Taylor, would like to say a few words."

"Shhhhh!" Jessi said, bits of candy practically flying out of her mouth. "I want to hear what Cody has to say."

"He's in our English class," I said, recognizing him as he took the stage with the other boys. He usually sat next to Steven, the boy who had helped me get to practice that first day. Cody and Jessi seemed pretty friendly in class. I'd noticed that Jessi seemed to prefer whispering to Cody rather than actually paying attention to the teacher!

"It's my absolute honor to represent the pride of Kentville Middle School," Cody began. Cody had on a dress shirt and a thin tie that had clearly been picked out to match the school's Kentville blue. He looked very mature and composed, especially compared to his rowdy teammates behind him, who were jostling one another and joking around while he talked.

Frida yawned. "Anybody else bored by all this?"

"Shhh," Jessi said. "Some of us are trying to listen!"

"Sheesh, okay," Frida said, surprised at Jessi's insistence. Then she lowered her voice to a whisper. "Someone's got a crush, huh?"

Cody talked for a few minutes more before turning the microphone over to the eighth-grade captain, Trey Bishop.

Looking at the stage, I spotted Steven. He caught my eye and gave me a shy smile.

"He's cute, right?" Jessi said. I blushed and looked away from the scene in front of me. I didn't want to be caught staring. "I love his little tie." Oh, she was talking about Cody.

It wasn't until after the pep rally, as we all walked back to class, that I realized nobody onstage had mentioned that *our* first game was that day too. So, correction: Kentville didn't just care about soccer—it cared about *boys'* soccer.

The girls' team? Not so much.

CHAPTER SIX

"Kicks, Kicks!" everyone on the bus chanted. We were about to leave for our first game. The pep rally, even though it had been for the boys, had gotten us fired up too. Or maybe it was the sugar from the candy they'd handed out. Either way we were pumped.

"Aren't you excited?" Emma was practically yelling in our faces. As soon as the bus pulled away from the school, Emma broke open a big bag of M&M's. She managed to spill half of them all over the floor. Her face turned bright red.

"Clean up in aisle four!" Zoe yelled.

We all laughed hysterically, surprised at Zoe's uncharacteristic zinger. When I smiled at Jessi, I noticed she looked upset.

"What's up?" I asked her, concerned.

"I left my notebook at the pep rally," she said. "I didn't

have my homework for math class. Which means I got a big fat zero."

"It's just one zero," I said, trying to cheer her up. "You'll make up for it."

Jessi sighed. "Never mind about me. How are you feeling, Co-captain?"

I dropped my voice. Mirabelle was sitting in the back of the bus with her friends, but I didn't want her to overhear me. "So why did you nominate me for co-captain? You'd be great at it."

"Too much responsibility," Jessi replied. "Besides, you're an awesome player, and we need somebody strong to stand up to Princess Mirabelle."

She smiled and I felt relieved to see her happy again. It had seemed weird to see her worried, since she was usually so upbeat.

"So, this is your favorite part about soccer, right?" I asked. Jessi looked confused.

"Getting to leave school early!" I joked.

She agreed. "Those are the best kind of school days!" She called across the aisle to Emma. "Hey, Emma, give me one of those M&Ms." She opened her mouth wide as Emma took aim.

We spent the ride to Victorton laughing while trying to toss M&M's into one another's mouths from across the aisle. Jessi was right—I liked school and all, but this was way better than being in class.

When we got to Victorton, just a short ride away, I looked for my mom, dad, and Maisie in the stands. I finally spotted them.

"Devin!" My dad called, waving with his free hand. In his other he was holding his video camera, just like always. Dad actually knew very little about soccer, but he tried to understand it. And he never missed a game, or the chance to record it on video. Last year, at the end of the season, he'd made the highlight video for our team. It had had slo-mo and been set to music and everything. It had been a hit at our team banquet.

I waved to my family and pointed them out to Jessi, who waved too. When she spotted the camera, she did a silly little dance. Maisie started cracking up. Jessi never missed an opportunity to ham it up. Then we headed to the visitors' bench to gear up.

Jessi reached into her bag and pulled out a colorful set of blue-and-orange plaid socks.

"These are so cool! Here's one of mine," I said, handing her one of my pink floral socks.

"What are you doing?" Zoe asked curiously.

"We're switching one sock, for luck," I explained. "Coach said we didn't have to wear uniform matching socks, so we're having some fun with it."

"I could use some luck too. Who wants to swap a sock with me?" Zoe asked. Of course, even Zoe's knee socks were totally fashionable: red, orange, purple, and cream stripes. They would have looked just as adorable with a skirt for school as they did with her soccer uniform. Frida came running over. "Fun!" she said. She had white socks with colorful polka dots all over them.

The seventh graders gathered around to see what was going on. A couple of the eighth graders smiled when they saw what was happening and came running over, socks in hand to join in.

"Stop." Mirabelle held her hand up. "This is so juvenile," she said, and sniffed.

The eighth-grade girls, shoulders slumped, walked away disappointed. I saw Grace shaking her head, but she didn't say anything. It didn't look like even the other eighth graders had the nerve to stand up to Mirabelle. I felt that maybe, as the co-captain, I should say something. But Mirabelle's fierce, angry eyes made me keep my mouth shut.

Jessi wasn't afraid of Mirabelle. She just rolled her eyes and stuck her tongue out as Mirabelle walked away. At least Mirabelle didn't try to stop the seventh graders from having fun.

"Wait. We have to put them on a special way too," Jessi said. "For good luck. Here, watch me." She made a big show of putting on her right sock first and wiggling her toes, and then she did the same with her left foot. We all followed suit.

"And then we put our left shoes on first," I added. "And you tie the right one last."

My hand went up and touched my pink headband. No

matter what, I would always keep the ritual I'd had with Kara. Too bad Mirabelle had stopped us from making a new one with all of the Kangaroos. I asked Jessi to snap a picture of me with my phone camera, and then I sent the pic off to Kara.

First game in California! I texted her.

Now I was ready.

As game time neared, I started to get the jitters. I hopped up and down, warming up my legs, and did a few stretches. Coach Flores gathered us into a large circle. "Girls, it's a beautiful day, so go out there and have fun! Everyone will have an equal chance to play. Eighth graders, you're up first. Then we'll sub in."

Wait, what? That made zero sense! And it didn't seem fair at all. If all the eighth graders always got to play first, some of us would never start a game.

Jessi threw up her hand to object. "Why can't we start too?"

"Don't worry, Jessi. Everyone will get the same playing time," Coach assured us, smiling. "It will be very fair. Fair and fun, words to live by!"

I didn't know what Coach Flores was thinking! I walked over to Jessi, Emma, and Zoe in a huff. "What is this all about?" I asked. "Why would Coach think it was a good idea to split us up by grade instead of starting out the best people in each position?"

Emma shrugged. "I guess she's trying to be fair?"

Mirabelle marched over to Coach Flores. "The eighth graders are short a player," she said curtly. "I guess it's not a surprise since you gave us such short notice about the game."

"How about Devin?" Coach Flores suggested, ignoring Mirabelle's snarky comment. "Since she's a captain?"

Mirabelle nodded. "Only if we can both play striker."

"As long as that's okay with the rest of the team." There went Coach Flores again, trying to make everyone happy.

"No, I can wait. It's okay," I said. "Let Jessi play." Mirabelle rolled her eyes at me.

"I'd rather wait too," Jessi said. Now none of the seventh graders wanted to start. The Kangaroos couldn't even get eleven players on the field!

Frida chimed in, "If people are volunteering, I don't need to play at all." *Great, even more of a mess.*

Finally Coach Flores stepped in. "All the eighth graders plus Devin, get out there. Everyone will have the same playing time," she repeated. It was the most decisive I'd seen Coach Flores yet.

I headed onto the field to face off against the Victorton Eagles.

With our pregame disorganization carrying onto the field, we quickly went down 2–0 before fifteen minutes had even gone by. Then Mirabelle managed to dance her way through the Victorton defense for an unassisted goal, but as a whole we looked terrible.

By the time the rest of the other seventh graders got

into the game, the score was 4–1 and we weren't threatening to come back.

Jessi came in to sub as striker for Mirabelle, and since she had been itching to play, she ran around like a wild horse set free. Using her insane speed, she had no trouble blowing by the slower Eagle players. I was up at striker too, and I was sure that if I could get her a good pass, a goal would be easy.

I eventually got the ball, and I looked for Jessi, who was jetting up the field. Concentrating, I lofted a perfect pass to her. She easily sprinted to get underneath it, zooming past the last Eagles defender.

The ref blew a sharp note on his whistle. "Offsides!" he yelled.

"Jessi!" Mirabelle barked from the sidelines. "Stop going offsides!"

"I don't need your help," Jessi shot back. But the next time I got the ball and passed it to Jessi, she didn't go offsides, and instead booted it right into the net.

Finally it was my turn to come off the field. Zoe took my spot as striker.

"Zoe, get to the ball," I encouraged her. "Don't be nervous!" But Zoe, her eyes darting to the crowd in the bleachers, drifted away when the ball came toward her.

"Zoe, get it together!" Mirabelle shrieked in frustration. Screaming at Zoe didn't help. It just made her more nervous.

Frida, in goal, was even worse, not even paying attention

as the ball made its way toward her. She was daydreaming about Shakespeare, the school play, or whatever dramatic thoughts occupied her mind. Keeping watch over the goal was obviously not one of her priorities. To make matters worse, Emma tripped over her own two feet, no ball anywhere near her, twice.

"Jeez, Emma, learn to walk, for crying out loud!" Mirabelle yelled. We had a lot of solid players, like seventh graders Jessi, Brianna, Sarah, and Anna, and eighth graders like Grace and Anjali, but they couldn't overcome the sloppiness of the rest of the team.

In the end, with only Jessi's and Mirabelle's scores, we lost to Victorton by three.

Mom and Dad met up with me before our team got on the bus. My dad wrapped me in a big bear hug.

"You did great," he said, ruffling my hair. "I'm so proud of you."

I frowned. "We were awful."

"It's a new team and only your first game," my mom said in a soothing voice. "You'll get better. Just be patient. Here, have some water," she added, handing me a bottle.

Maisie smiled up at me. "I like your socks!

I gave her a quick hug before climbing onto the bus.

On the ride home everyone was a little bummed out— except for Emma, that is, who was still full of positive energy.

Emma leaned over the seat she was sitting in with Zoe to talk to me and Jessi. "Aw, don't look so sad. It's only a game! But I know just the thing to fix it."

"What's that?" Jessi asked.

"A sleepover!" Emma said. "Tomorrow night, my house. Zoe's coming too!" Emma said.

"Awesome!" I said. My first sleepover in my new town, with my new group of friends! Losing the game hurt, but this went a long way to make up for it.

CHAPTER SEVEN

Emma's house was in a private gated community, and as Dad drove me slowly around early Saturday afternoon, looking for her exact house number, we gawked as each house we went by got bigger and bigger. A guard at the gatehouse had even given us a map of the place, in case we got lost.

I was all smiles in the car. After only my first week of school, I had made friends and was on my way to a sleepover. I wish I had known I was going to meet Jessi, Emma, and Zoe before the first day of school. I would have been so much less nervous!

"Fancy," Dad said when we finally pulled up to Emma's mansion. Palm trees lined the big circular driveway, and a fountain splashed loudly in the middle. I couldn't even tell exactly how many stories the house was, or how wide around it went, as the building extended out of view. Emma lived in an absolute castle.

After my dad parked and we got out of the car, I grabbed my heavy sleepover bag and we walked up to ring the doorbell. As we waited at the oversize wooden door, Dad joked, "Don't touch anything."

A moment later the door swung open and Mrs. Kim's round friendly face greeted us. She had on a flowery apron, and her graying hair was short and curled. "Devin, we're so happy you could make it," she said.

"Thank you for inviting her, and if she causes you any trouble, just toss her into the fountain," Dad said with a laugh.

"Bye, Dad." I gave him a quick hug and ushered him away.

Once I was inside, Emma appeared. "Thanks for coming," she said. "Zoe and Jessi are here already. They're out back. Take your shoes off and come on in."

Emma led me from the foyer into a gigantic kitchen, where a group of ladies was preparing food. "These are my mom's friends and some of my aunts," Emma said, introducing me around. Then we picked our way through another room filled with people, this time a living room outfitted with a huge flat screen television.

"Move, move!" they screamed at us.

Emma attempted to duck and ended up tripping over someone's sneakers. She landed on her rear end on the floor, laughing as the room broke into applause. I helped her up, and she took a bow as everyone laughed.

Emma gigged before explaining, "My brothers and

our cousins all come here on the weekends. My family is obsessed with sports—especially soccer. We watch everything." Just then someone on the TV scored, and the room exploded in cheers. "KO-RE-A, KO-RE-A!" they chanted as we were caught in a celebratory tornado. It was high fives and fist bumps all around.

I totally understood now where Emma got all her enthusiasm from. It was obviously built into her DNA! We managed to make our way through the noisy television room. Emma slid open a glass door leading outside.

"You brought your swimsuit, right?" Emma asked, taking us into her backyard. I couldn't even answer her because the sight of her pool made me speechless. It was humongous, and edged in dark stones instead of the usual concrete curbing. Over at the far end of the pool, a water slide curled upward, all the way toward the roof of the house. Once, when our family went on vacation, the resort we stayed at had a pool like that. To live here would be like being on vacation all the time. But I couldn't help wondering whether it was safe to have a giant slide in your backyard when your daughter was as clumsy as Emma.

Zoe was next to the pool, lounging like a mini-model. Her strawberry-blond hair had been cut into a super-stylish pixie cut, the bangs long and swept across the front from left to right. She was flipping through a magazine and wearing sunglasses that were half the size of her face, even though she was in the shade.

My power of speech returned to me. "When did you

do that to your hair?" I exclaimed, making my way over to get a closer look. "It looks incredible!"

"Thanks! My mom took me this morning," she said. "I'm still getting used to it." It must have taken Zoe a lot of inner confidence to pull off some of her looks, which was surprising, given how shy she was.

"Where's Jessi?" Emma asked.

From above us we heard Jessi's kamikaze yell as she barreled down the slide and flew off the edge, cannon-balling into the water. She landed with a huge splash.

She climbed out of the water and gave me a big, wet hug.

"Hey!" I exclaimed, laughing as I looked down at my now wet clothes. "I don't even have to bother changing into my suit now!"

But I did change, in a fancy cabana next to the pool. After I had my suit on, I raced over to the pool and jumped in. Zoe had gotten off her lounge chair and was floating around on a raft, obviously trying to keep her new hairdo dry. Emma was floating on her back next to her.

"You've got to try the slide!" Jessi said, and we both raced up the stairs. As we stood at the top, I felt my tummy start to churn. It was really high.

"Come on!" Jessi yelled, and she slid down again, screaming the entire way. I heard a loud splash as she hit the water.

Here goes nothing, I thought as I sat down at the top of the slide. I pushed off, and my body went whoosh! I careened into the water next to Jessi.

"Isn't that awesome?" she asked, her brown eyes shining.

"Yes, but I think my stomach is still up there." I pointed to the top of the slide. "Wow, Emma has a really cool house."

"It's the best. We have lots of sleepovers here," Jessi said. "I hope I'll be able to come to more."

"Why?" I asked as I saw the smile fade from her face.

"My parents almost didn't let me come today," Jessi explained. "They're worried about my schoolwork. If I don't get my grades up, this might be my last sleepover party for a while."

"If you ever need any help, just ask me," I said. "My friend Kara and I used to study together all the time."

Jessi smiled. "Thanks."

Then Mrs. Kim called us inside for some food. There was a long table filled with ribs, potato salad, and cold noodles. There were also delicious-looking cupcakes.

"Let's take our plates to the game room. They'll be screaming over that soccer game for hours," Emma said, leading us to another part of the house. When she slid open the door, I could see that behind it was yet another gigantic television, plus a pool table, a foosball table, and a wall of DVDs and board games.

We settled into the big, comfy couches, eating Mrs. Kim's delicious Korean food.

"Ugh, food coma," Zoe said as she finished up her plate.

"That always happens when we come here," Jessi said happily. "Mrs. Kim always has the best snacks!"

I made a mental note to myself to make sure my mom had something other than kale chips and green smoothies if my friends ever came over to my house for a sleepover.

We all sat comfortably together for a while before the conversation turned to the team.

"So, what do you guys think of Coach Flores?" I asked, curious. "I've never had a coach like her before!"

"She's so nice," Emma said. "But sometimes I think she treats us like we're a bunch of babies. Did you see my loud family? I can handle a little healthy competition."

"The team is so disorganized," Jessi complained. "It's like a free-for-all whenever we hit the field."

Zoe frowned. "I wish I was more of a help on the team."

Emma laughed. "You can't help it!" she said to Zoe. Then Emma turned to us and said, "You should have seen her last year before our group presentation for Spanish class. She threw up in the girls' bathroom."

"Hey!" Zoe said with a laugh. "That's not funny! Okay, maybe it was a little."

"Did that really happen?" I asked, astonished.

"Yeah," she said. "People watching me does that to me sometimes, when there's a lot of pressure. Stage fright, I guess." She shrugged.

I felt bad for Zoe. I couldn't imagine getting that nervous about playing. The soccer field had always been where I felt the most confident. Plus, Zoe had real talent when she felt like no one was watching her. It seemed like a shame, really.

"All you need to do is stop worrying," Emma said encouragingly. "Then you'll be great!"

Zoe let out a big sigh. "Maybe."

"We've got lots of problems as a team, not just Zoe's nerves," I said sadly. "There's no structure. It's all chaos when we hit the field. I know I'm a co-captain, but really it's up to Coach Flores to step up and whip us into shape."

Jessi got a mischievous grin on her face. "How about you and your fellow co-captain have a talk with her?"

I shuddered at the thought of doing anything with Mirabelle.

"I'm still surprised the eighth graders voted her as captain," I said.

"I think it's a combination of respect and fear," Zoe said. "She is an awesome player."

"But not all of them seemed happy about it," Jessi reminded her.

"You know what I was also wondering about?" I said. "We've got a game coming up with Pinewood. Didn't you say that Mirabelle is friends with some of the girls on that team?"

Jessi nodded. "Yep, they are her bffs!"

"Do you think she would try to sabotage us, so Pinewood would win?" I wondered.

Jessi, Emma, and Zoe all started laughing. "Um, the way we're playing, no sabotage is needed," Jessi said.

I chuckled too. "I guess you're right."

"And Pinewood is the best team around," Emma added. "They don't need much help."

Jessi rolled her eyes. "Knowing Mirabelle, she wants to show off in front of her friends. She'd be, like, sooooo embarrassed if our team was a total disaster."

The team's troubles seemed like too much. I was tired of thinking about it. I eyed the foosball table. "Want to play some foosball to work off some of that food?"

"I'll play with Devin. Jessi, you and Zoe can pair up," Emma chimed in.

It turned out Emma was a foosball queen. She defended our goal like it was nobody's business.

When we were winning 10–0, Jessi and Zoe finally forfeited.

"We give up!" said Zoe. "Have mercy!"

We were doubled over laughing when Mrs. Kim came downstairs. "You girls hungry for s'mores?" she asked.

We all looked around at one another questioningly, smiles slowly dawning on our faces. Could we actually manage to stuff down more delicious food? Of course we could.

"You bet!" Emma called out to her mom.

Emma took us out by the pool again, where her mom had set up a small fire in their wrought-iron fire pit for us to make s'mores. The sky was clear and there were stars everywhere.

"Do you know about the dance next Friday night? We

should all meet here. We can get dressed together," Emma suggested. "And one of my brothers can drive us."

"There's a dance?" Zoe asked.

"Yup," said Jessi. "The theme is Neon Nights. Sounds pretty cool, right?" She got a dreamy look in her eyes. "I wonder if Cody will be there."

I was kind of wondering if Steven would be there too, but I didn't say anything out loud. Instead I looked up at the sky. "Look, a shooting star!" I pointed.

"Make a wish!" Emma cried out. We all squeezed our eyes shut, wishing with all our might.

I wished that the Kicks would start playing better. I had a feeling I wasn't the only one who made that wish. We all wanted the team to be good. With everything such a mess, wishing seemed like the only thing we could do now.

When it was almost eleven and time to go to sleep, Mrs. Kim brought out some hot chocolate, four sleeping bags, and some pillows. We fell asleep with the whole galaxy above us, and Jessi's soft snoring as a sound track.

CHAPTER EIGHT

Wishing didn't work. Things weren't getting any better for the Kangaroos. In the locker room before our home game against the Newton Tigers that very next Monday, Mirabelle gave her version of a pep talk.

"You guys stink!" she yelled. "Get it together this game. You got to want to win! Got it?" she said threateningly. Some captain. What was she going to do, beat us all up if we lost? Jessi slammed her locker shut loudly and shot Mirabelle a glance that could have melted an ice cube. Mirabelle took the hint and shut up before stalking out of the locker room.

The trouble we were having off the field spilled onto it. There was no sense of teamwork. At the game only the seventh graders participated in the sock swap, while Mirabelle glowered in anger. Coach Flores started all the eighth graders again, filling in with the seventh graders as needed. Once again the strategy didn't work.

Zoe still hadn't gotten over her soccer stage fright, and Frida hardly paid any attention to the game at all. As a Tiger came in with a low, fast kick to the side of the goal, Frida stood to the side, her eyes closed while her lips were moving. What was she doing? Not watching the game, obviously. The ball flew in without our goalie even noticing.

Mirabelle's screams could be heard across the entire field. "Frida, pay attention!" she hollered, her face turning red with anger.

Emma had a good run going with the ball, but once again tripped and went splat on the field, leaving the ball wide open for an interception. Grace and Anjali, two of the eighth graders, played a great game. Grace's quiet intensity was an asset on the field. For the seventh grade, Jessi, Brianna, Sarah, and Anna were solid, good players, and I tried my best. But we just weren't connecting. Once again we couldn't overcome the chaos. The game was a total disaster. The Kentville Kangaroos were now 0–2 to start the season.

"What were you doing out there?" Mirabelle asked Frida after the game, exasperated.

"I was practicing my Academy Awards acceptance speech," Frida said defiantly. She wasn't afraid of Mirabelle. "It seemed like a better way to spend my time."

Mirabelle rolled her eyes. "Useless," she muttered under her breath. There was nothing she could do. We were stuck with Frida as goalie. Nobody wanted the job, and since Frida didn't even want to play, she didn't care what position she was in.

Mirabelle turned her intense gaze on me. "Devin, we captains need to talk." She stalked off to the side of the field. Not knowing what else to do, I followed her.

"We can't afford to keep losing," Mirabelle told me. "We're not going to make the end-of-season tournament like this," she continued. "I want us to put on a good showing, especially for the Pinewood game."

"I heard you had some friends on the Pinewood team," I said innocently.

Mirabelle stared at me. "Jessi tell you that?"

I nodded. Oops. I hoped I hadn't stirred something up.

She glared at me. "Don't listen to everything Jessi says. But it is true, I do have some friends at Pinewood, and I have to make a good impression at that game. Devin, you want to win too, right?" Mirabelle stared at me intensely.

"Of course I want to win," I replied. *But you need strategy to win,* I wanted to add. And as far as strategy went, we had none.

"Good. It's obvious Coach doesn't care much about making the team better, so as captains it's our responsibility." Mirabelle had a look on her face that would stop a rampaging bull in its steps.

"I know," I said. Mirabelle definitely wasn't my favorite person, but I had to agree with her. "I don't get it."

"You know she used to play college soccer, right?" Mirabelle asked.

"She did?" That totally surprised me. "No way! You'd never know. She doesn't teach us much of anything."

Mirabelle shrugged. "I know. Anyway, maybe the better players, like you and me, should play more minutes." It was flattering that Mirabelle thought I was on her level. Or close to it.

"And I think Jessi and Brianna have been great too," I offered.

"Jessi? Oh, come on," Mirabelle said dismissively. "She doesn't try hard enough. Trust me, I know her. We used to be friends."

"She told me you guys grew up together," I said cautiously.

"Jessi used to be better than me at soccer. I mean, sports always came super-easy to her. But when I started getting better and joined the travel team, she got jealous." Mirabelle shrugged.

That didn't sound like the story I'd heard, but I kept my mouth shut.

"Anyway, we should talk to Coach about this playing-time stuff," Mirabelle said. "You gotta back me up when I say the better players deserve to play more."

"Okay," I said hesitantly. "Isn't that unfair to everyone else on the team, though?" I was thinking about what Mirabelle's solution would mean for the rest of the team—for players like Emma, in particular, who loved the game but weren't necessarily stars in the making.

"Look, you're a captain," Mirabelle said. "This is what captains do. We help the team make decisions," Mirabelle continued, her voice rising. "It's for the good of the team."

"All right, all right, I understand," I said, backing down. It would be nice to try to win a game or two. But was it worth the price of fairness?

After the next practice Mirabelle and I went to go talk to Coach Flores. Jessi raised her eyebrows as she saw us walking off together. I shrugged helplessly. Mirabelle kept lecturing me all the way to Coach's office. "Remember, we have a goal here. We'll make it happen if we stick together. Got it?"

"Sure," I said, rushing to keep up with her as she speed-walked down the hall. Something about this didn't feel right.

When we arrived at Coach Flores's door, Mirabelle breezed right in without knocking.

"Hello there, girls," Coach Flores said, her usual grin plastered on her face. "Take a seat."

"That's okay," Mirabelle said. "This will just take a minute. Devin and I, as co-captains, thought that it would be better for our next game if *we* got to choose the positions and substitutions," she said, her voice sugary sweet. "Just for one game, to try it out. I think it would really help us learn responsibility and teamwork."

I did a mental eye roll. Puh-leaze! Coach might be too nice, but even she wouldn't buy Mirabelle's sugar-and-spice act. Or would she?

Coach hesitated. For a second I was sure she wouldn't go for it. I mean, she was all about equal playing time for everyone. "You guys decided this?" she asked, looking at both of us. We nodded together.

"Well, if you girls want to try doing the lineups, I'm not against it. Just make sure everyone agrees to it and people are enjoying themselves. And above all, be fair." She emphasized the last word.

"Taken care of! We already asked them. They're all very excited about it," Mirabelle said with a winning smile. It was a flat-out lie. My jaw dropped open, but I couldn't get the words to come out of my mouth to contradict Mirabelle.

Coach raised her eyebrows, looking surprised. "If everyone agreed," she said, "then I'm all for it. It's nice to see you two captains being proactive."

I felt a little sick inside. This wasn't right, but I didn't know what to do. To tell the truth, I was afraid to stand up to Mirabelle.

When we left Coach Flores's office, Mirabelle was crowing. "See how easy that was? Now we have a shot at winning. I'll tell you who I think we should play. Then we'll tell them before our next game."

So much for being co-captains.

I was starting to get the idea that Mirabelle was very

good at getting what she wanted—no matter what the cost. I felt guilty that I hadn't stood up to her. I should have said something to Coach Flores! Would all my new friends be mad at me?

CHAPTER nine

I felt totally nervous and guilty about our new lineup strategy. Well, make that Mirabelle's lineup strategy. Apparently as co-captain my job was to stand there and nod while Mirabelle did all the talking.

Mom, Dad, and Maisie were waiting for me in the parking lot. We drove home together, with Maisie complaining loudly.

"You promised me I'd get a juice box at Devin's next soccer game," she protested. "If I have to go to all these games, I want a treat!"

My mom sighed. "I forgot to pick some up. I told you that." Even though juice, soda, and sugary snacks were forbidden as a general rule, we did get them as treats and for special occasions.

I wished the biggest problem in my life were the lack of a juice box. I sighed loudly and just stared out the window, not saying anything.

We pulled into the driveway. My mom and dad exchanged looks. "Maisie, come in and help me set the table for dinner," Mom said.

Maisie, still grumbling, followed Mom into the house.

Dad grabbed a soccer ball out of the trunk. "Want to kick the ball around a little bit before we eat?" he suggested.

I shrugged. "I guess."

We walked to the backyard. Dad lobbed the ball toward me, and I halfheartedly kicked it. We kicked the ball back and forth for a while in silence, my dad giving me time to unwind.

"So, Devin, are you ready to tell me about whatever is bothering you?" he finally asked.

I let out a big breath of air and kicked the ball so hard, it went flying over the fence and into the neighbor's yard.

My dad grinned at me. "I bet that felt good."

It did. And before I knew it, the entire saga of Mirabelle and Coach Flores came pouring out.

"What if everyone hates me?" I wailed as I finished telling him everything that had happened.

Dad wrapped his arms around me, giving me a big hug. "Relax," he said. "Nobody is going to hate you. It sounds like this Mirabelle is a strong personality. I'm sure all your friends understand that."

Strong personality. I laughed to myself. That was one way to describe her!

"And I understand the motivation behind why she did what she did, even if her methods weren't sound," Dad continued. "Coach Flores needs to give the team more direction. I don't blame Mirabelle for wanting to take charge. Do you want me to talk to the coach about this?"

"No!" I said, my eyes wide. That would be so embarrassing. And the last thing I needed was Mirabelle's wrath for having my dad tattle on her.

"Okay. Then let's look at the facts," Dad said. "According to you, Mirabelle is not that nice. But she wants the team to be better. So don't worry about her lineup strategy until you see it. It might be something you can agree with her on. If you don't think everyone is getting a fair share of playing time, you'll have to say something. Do you think you can do that?" My dad cupped my chin with his hand and looked into my eyes. "You're a natural-born leader, Devin. And people really like you. Don't forget that. You don't have to be afraid of Mirabelle."

I felt myself standing up straighter. My dad always knew what to say to make me feel better.

After dinner that night Kara called. It was like her best friend supersense was tingling, and she just knew I needed her.

"I am so glad to hear your voice!" I gushed when I answered the phone.

"What's up?" Kara asked.

I filled her in on the Mirabelle drama and told her what my dad had said.

"He's right," Kara agreed. "You don't have to be afraid of her. She's just a bully. If you stand up to her, she'll back down."

Kara and my dad were right. If I had to, I would totally stand up to Mirabelle!

I'm usually a good student, but I found it pretty hard to concentrate during class on Wednesday, knowing I had to face Mirabelle and the Pinewood Panthers that afternoon.

The day dragged on, but finally I was sitting in my last class of the day, English, next to Jessi. Mr. Williams was writing on the board, and I was taking notes when I felt something brush against my arm. I looked down. A paper airplane had landed on my desk.

I looked around, confused. Where had it come from? I slowly opened it up. It was a note!

Good luck against the Panthers today. I'll be there cheering you on! —*Steven*

I glanced up. Steven looked at me and grinned. I felt my cheeks turn pink. I mouthed "Thanks" to him before looking away.

Of course, Jessi had seen the entire thing. She raised her eyebrows at me. Great. I knew she'd ask me all about it. And not only did I have to worry about Mirabelle and the Panthers, but now I had to think about Steven watching from the stands too!

Even though their school was only half an hour away, it felt like a different universe before our bus even pulled onto campus. Cars were lined up around the block, slowly rolling past the security gate and into the parking lot. What were they all here for? A carnival?

"*This* is all for a girls' soccer game?" I wondered.

"They take their soccer seriously at Pinewood," Zoe said.

As our bus passed the Pinewood fans, some of them honked their horns at us, and they smiled and waved little flags. "They seem nice," I said to nobody in particular.

Jessi snorted. "They've beat us five years in a row, so it is pretty easy for them to be nice to us. We're like human sacrifices for them."

Zoe laughed nervously. She still hadn't gotten over her stage fright, and I could tell that if anyone felt like a human soccer sacrifice, it was her!

But Emma wasn't nervous at all. "I can't wait to play," she said, her eyes shining as she looked out the window. "My entire family is coming to cheer me on. Hopefully I won't fall on my face this time," she said with a laugh.

Brianna sat next to Anna, her head buried in a book. "Earth to Brianna!" Anna called. Brianna didn't even notice, she was concentrating so hard. "She's got a test tomorrow," Anna explained.

"Gotta keep up that four-point-oh!" Sarah chimed from the seat in front of them. Frida sat next to her, looking glumly out the window.

"I could be at an audition for a nationwide commercial today," she complained, slumping farther into the ratty old bus seat. "But no. My mother is all like, 'You need to have a normal childhood, blah, blah, blah.' Doesn't she get it? I'm not normal!"

Everyone burst out laughing at that, and even Frida had to join in. Soon we were driving onto the Pinewood campus. It looked like a superfancy private school. Each of the school's buildings seemed to be made out of silvery metal, and the main building had giant windows that reflected the afternoon sunlight. In comparison Kentville Middle School looked like a bunch of dirt huts.

When we got off the bus and onto the field, the stands were filled with at least two hundred people, all chattering excitedly and all wearing purple and gold, Pinewood's colors. There was a drum line in the front, leading their fans in singing and chanting. "Knock, knock, guess who? The Panthers are gonna stomp on you!" Then everyone in the stands stomped twice, and the crowd cheered wildly.

Our cheering section, over in the away-team bleachers, looked kind of pathetic. Mom, Dad, and Maisie were cheering us on. I noticed Maisie was triumphantly holding a juice box in her hand. Emma's immediate family was there, along with a lot of uncles, cousins, and aunts, but all the Kims and their friends couldn't compare to the number of people crammed onto the bursting Pinewood side of the stands. I was continuing to scan the Kicks' cheering section, looking for Steven, when I felt Jessi nudge me in the side with her elbow. Of course she'd wanted the lowdown on the note as soon as class was over, so I had told her everything.

"Is that Cody with Steven?" she whispered loudly.

I spotted not only Steven and Cody but the rest of the boys' soccer team too.

Steven saw me and raised his hand, waving and smiling. Cody joined him. Jessi and I waved back. But no one else on the boys' team looked happy to see us.

"Their coach made them come," Frida said when she spotted the team. "A couple of the guys are in my Spanish class, and they were complaining about it today. I told them I didn't want to go either, so they should just shut their traps." Boy, was she grumpy.

"Well, I guess we'll just have to show them how awesome we actually are, right?" Jessi said as she lifted her chin and crossed her arms.

"Uh, sure," I said. I thought Jessi's crush was making her a little goofy. And a little forgetful of how our team had been playing.

My stomach began to clench up. This time the butterflies brought a rock band with them. Not only did I have Steven's eyes on me, but also what looked like the eyes of a million Panther fans. And I had to worry about Mirabelle and her lineup, too. I looked over at Zoe, who was standing next to me, nervously chewing on her nails. Her face was pale. She looked like I felt.

"You okay?" I asked. She barely nodded. I had to cheer her up, and myself, too.

"Sock swap!" I yelled. All the seventh graders came running, but once again Mirabelle held the eighth graders back, loudly calling us a "bunch of babies."

The seventh graders didn't care, though. We all stood in a circle, and each of us handed a sock to the person standing on our left. Then we sat down on the grass and put them on the way Jessi had shown us, giggling the entire time. After we were finished, I touched my hand to my pink headband. I was ready to play!

Just then the cheering intensified and the Pinewood team appeared. The Panthers jogged onto the field in three perfectly straight lines, wearing matching warm-up suits. "They can't be middle schoolers," I said. I flashed back to seeing Mirabelle for the first time, how intimidating she'd looked. The Pinewood team was like a pack of Mirabelles, a team of Amazons. No wonder she was friends with them. She fit right in.

"Devin, let's go," Mirabelle called to me. It was the captain's meeting at midfield. I rushed to catch up with her long strides. Three of the Panthers approached, all of them holding hands in solidarity. When Mirabelle saw that, she slowed down to grab my hand too. "Smile," she whispered to me. Grudgingly I made myself put on a small smile. *She is so fake*, I thought as her hand clamped down on mine like a steel trap.

"Pinewood, call heads or tails," the referee said, a coin in one hand and a ball tucked underneath his other arm.

"Heads," one of the Panthers captains said. Their uniforms were so pretty. All white with purple stripes running down the side. It looked like their uniforms had gold flecks on them too. Our blue away uniforms suddenly felt like trash bags, especially mine, with its masking tape on the back.

The coin came up tails. "We'll defend first," Mirabelle said, without consulting me.

"Let's have a clean game," the ref said. "Go ahead and shake hands, girls."

We cheerfully exchanged "good lucks," and as we walked away, Mirabelle said, "I want to win."

"Sure," I said. We all did.

"No, you don't understand. I *need* to win. Which means Emma can't play."

I stopped in my tracks. "What?"

Mirabelle stopped too. "You need to tell Coach that Emma won't play."

Why single out Emma? There were lots of reasons our team wasn't doing well, and it wasn't fair to Emma to pin all the blame on her. The team needed to work together. It wasn't one player's responsibility. *Maybe Mirabelle singled Emma out because she's such good friends with Jessi,* I thought. After all, Jessi had warned me that Mirabelle wasn't nice to any of Jessi's friends. My stomach knotted up. The butterflies were back, and this time they were doing some Olympic-level gymnastics. Imagining myself standing up to Mirabelle, and actually doing it, were two very different things. As she looked at me with her laserlike eyes, I almost crumbled. But I thought of what my dad had said to me and Emma's excitement on the bus. I reached deep inside and found my courage.

I stood up straight and looked Mirabelle dead in the eyes. "No way. Emma *is* playing. Her entire family is here. And she's my friend. I won't take her out of the game," I insisted.

"She's going to make us lose." Mirabelle was practically shouting.

"We're a team!" I shouted back."How can one person make us lose? We win *and* lose together." I held her gaze and didn't blink. "Emma is playing."

"Fine," Mirabelle said angrily, stalking away. "You're in charge of subbing her out when she messes up."

I let out a deep breath as I walked back to the rest of the team on the sidelines. I had done it! But it wasn't over yet. I watched as Mirabelle got ready to assign starting positions, and I was ready to jump in if she left Emma out. All the forwards and defenders were eighth graders, except for Brianna. "Devin, Jessi, Emma. You three can play midfield. All right, let's go," Mirabelle said. She had listened to me! Standing up to Mirabelle had worked.

Once the game started, however, it became clear that Emma was the least of our problems. Pinewood was just too good. After the kickoff one of their players streaked right through the middle of the field untouched. We weren't even set up yet. Pass. Pass. Score. It was that simple for them.

Mirabelle got our kickoff and tried to do the same thing. Pinewood's players were much more disciplined than ours, though, and three of them swarmed her, forcing Mirabelle to kick the ball out of bounds.

Their ensuing sidelines toss-in cleared a third of the field, the ball soaring right over Emma's head. The Panthers were there, though, and they scored again. They didn't just have first-rate facilities and uniforms—their play was first-rate too. Pinewood made us look like a joke.

"Jessi!" Mirabelle yelled when she managed to take control of the ball again. Mirabelle voluntarily passing to Jessi? She must have really wanted to win. Jessi was open on the flank, but she wasn't paying attention to where the last Pinewood defender was. Instead of slowing down to prevent offsides, she sped up.

The referee blew his whistle. "Offsides!" A scoring chance evaporated.

Pinewood scored again on a corner kick. 3–0.

Mirabelle was getting angry. You could see it on her face.

"Get the ball, Devin!" Mirabelle screamed at me. I was trying! I managed to steal a pass. "Go, go, go!" Mirabelle yelled as I charged up the field.

Where was I supposed to go with it? No one was open, and I was too far back to score. Mirabelle's losing her cool was throwing me off my game.

I kicked the ball as hard I could downfield, just to get rid of it. Even though I was supposed to be a midfielder, I was now basically full-time defense. Everyone had shifted back a line, except for Jessi. She was stationed all the way up the field, the loneliest Kangaroo. I guess if we ever got a chance to score, she would be poised to do so.

The Pinewood fans in the stands started doing their stomping thing on the bleachers again, and I was getting a serious headache. "There's a mercy rule in soccer, right?" Anna huffed.

"Maybe we can come back," I said hopefully.

"Maybe we can forfeit," Anna suggested.

Another ball came flying back down our way. Anna tried to slide tackle someone, but she missed. Now there were two Panthers for me to stop. I managed to intercept their pass and knock the ball toward Emma.

Pressured by another Panthers player on the wing, Emma turned her back, shielding the ball. *Good. Now get it out of here!* I thought. Emma cleared some space by swinging her arms wildly, and, facing the goal, she pulled her leg back for a huge kick.

But *our* goalie, Frida, was right in front of her, and Frida held out her arms as her eyes got really big. *Emma had no idea she was facing her own team's goal.* If I could have frozen time, I would have right then.

BOOM. Emma blasted the kick of her life. Right on target, right past our goalie, right into our own goal.

The crowd completely stopped chanting. Nobody moved. For the first time since we'd arrived at Pinewood, there was silence. Emma gasped, her hands flying to her open mouth as she realized what had just happened.

I felt terrible, but I couldn't help thinking: *I should have listened to Mirabelle.*

Breaking the spell, an appreciative clap started from the Pinewood stands. The clap grew into thunderous applause, all directed at Emma. It wasn't even mean-spirited. They just felt bad for us. Some even yelled words of encouragement: "Don't worry. You'll do better next time!"

Inexplicably Emma took a bow, which generated more applause. I was shocked at Pinewood's positivity. What kind of people were nice to you as they annihilated you? Monsters, that's who.

At halftime the score was 6–0, including Emma's massive mistake.

Mirabelle grabbed my arm as we gathered in the visitors' locker room. "I hope you're happy," she hissed into my ear. "You friend made us look like fools out there." She let go and stalked off angrily to the other side of the room.

I sighed. How could anyone have predicted that Emma would do that?

Coach Flores didn't have much to say. Even her usual sunny smile was dimmed. "We're doing okay out there. Not the best, but okay. Just keep hustling and try to have fun. Everyone who hasn't played yet, let's get in there." The girls on the bench weren't that excited to join the slaughter. When we got our only goal in the second half, by Mirabelle, I couldn't even celebrate. For the rest of the game I tried not to look miserable while sitting on the bench.

As the game wound down, the Pinewood fans

serenaded us with the losers song—"Who do we appreciate? Kangaroos! Kangaroos!" Frida summed it up perfectly: "At least in theater no one applauds when you mess up."

Feeling defeated, I decided to head home with my parents instead of taking the bus back. When my family was walking back to our car after the game, my mom and dad offered to take me for frozen yogurt to help ease the sting of that awful loss. I was all for drowning my sorrows with an extra helping of crushed cookies, and peanut butter cups on top. As I climbed into the backseat, I saw Mirabelle and her dad standing with the Panthers coach. Her eyes glanced around and landed on me for just a second. Then she just as quickly looked away, an almost guilty look in her eyes. Huh, I thought. That wasn't like Mirabelle. I wondered what she was up to now.

CHAPTER TEN

"Nice goal on Wednesday!" one of the eighth-grade soccer boys shouted sarcastically at Emma as she, Jessi, Zoe, and I walked by him on Friday on our way to our usual court-yard lunch spot. He put his fist up in the air in mock salute.

I couldn't help flinching even though he wasn't talking to me.

"Thank you, thank you," Emma called back while curtsying. "My best goal ever!"

"How are you not embarrassed?" I asked Emma. I wanted to be embarrassed for her. "You're acting like it's just a big joke. And I know it was an accident, but we lost the game."

"What's the big deal?" Emma said. "It's not like we would have won anyway, and honestly, I figure it's better to just embrace my stupid mistake than feel too terrible about it. Plus, we all lost together, right? My brother said soccer is the ultimate team game."

"I guess you're right," I said, impressed. I really admired Emma. I would have wanted to crawl under a rock or pretend I was sick and skip school. But she didn't let it bother her.

As we settled into our spots and began to eat our lunches, Brianna, Sarah, and Anna showed up. "Hey, Devin!" Brianna called. "Thanks for inviting us."

"We're a team!" I smiled. The game had been awful, it was true, but standing up to Mirabelle had given me new confidence. My dad was right. Our team needed leadership, but not the nasty kind offered by Mirabelle. I wanted to bring us together. It was time for me to start acting like a captain, not Mirabelle's puppet.

"What happened between you and Mirabelle at the game?" Anna asked, her brown eyes curious. "I saw her grab you in the locker room."

"You know Mirabelle," I said, trying to play it off. I hadn't told the other girls about how Mirabelle hadn't wanted Emma to play.

Sarah rolled her eyes. "There is no making that girl happy!"

Jessi was once again furiously scribbling in her notebook, not paying attention to our conversation.

"More last-minute homework?" I asked her.

She sighed. "I totally forgot about the Spanish assignment, and I'm still doing terrible in math."

"I told you I would help you!" I reminded her. "Anytime! All you have to do is ask."

"Devin is in eighth-grade algebra," Zoe reminded her. "You couldn't get a better tutor!"

"It's all just so boring!" Jessi complained. I could understand. Jessi was always full of energy. It was hard to picture her sitting quietly studying. She always needed to be doing something.

"But you can't just not do the work for the class," Brianna said, shocked. The more I got to know her, the more I realized she was a typical overachiever. Straight As in everything and always rushing off to one extracurricular after another. You could tell Brianna would never dream of watching a reality TV show instead of doing her homework.

Jessi looked embarrassed. "Let's just change the subject," she said. "How about the dance tonight? Aren't you guys excited?"

We all nodded. "Definitely," I said. "And I overheard Cody say to Steven in English yesterday about how he's going to the dance." I gave her a sly look.

"You're making that up. If he said that, then why didn't I hear him?" said Jessi. She threw a pretzel at me.

"It couldn't have been because you were concentrating on your work!" I exclaimed with a laugh as I tossed the pretzel back at her.

And once again we all started laughing. I couldn't believe that I had been in school for a little less than two weeks, and here I was surrounded by friends. I had come a long way from hiding in the bathroom stall.

CHAPTER ELEVEN

We met up at Emma's house before the dance to get ready. When I got there, Emma and Zoe were already crowded into her bathroom, playing around with some makeup.

"Whoa, you look great," I said to Emma. She was out of her usual uniform of shapeless hoodies and shorts, and had on a light blue sleeveless dress with white polka dots, and a white patent leather belt around her waist. Her hair was tied up into its usual bun, but she had added tiny silk flowers for decoration.

"Zoe helped me pick the dress out," Emma said. Zoe was on her tippy toes, looking into the mirror and fussing with the front of her hair. She had on a slim dress with a Peter Pan collar, and her legs were wrapped in dark floral tights. As always she looked like she had just stepped out of a magazine. Zoe waved at me from her reflection as she perfected her bangs.

"My mom is demanding that we take pictures before we leave," Emma continued.

"Awesome," I said. "I need a cute picture of the four of us."

"Here, let me do your makeup," Zoe said, pulling me in front of the mirror. Lip gloss, mascara, and eye shadow were littered around the countertop. It looked like she had borrowed everything she could get her hands on from her older sisters. She put mascara on my eyelashes, a tiny bit of peach blush on my cheeks, and topped it all off with some sparkly light pink lip gloss.

I gazed at myself in the mirror, unused to seeing myself with makeup on. "It looks so natural!" I said.

Jessi showed up after we had gotten ready, just in time for pictures. She had on a silver sequin top and black pants, and her hair was pulled to one side.

"Fashionably late, as usual, Jessi," Emma teased.

Jessi looked glum. "My mom almost didn't let me come. My math teacher gave her a call this afternoon." She shook her head. "But let's forget about that. You guys look fantastic!"

"So do you!" I said, and we gathered in front of Emma's fireplace for photos.

My soccer pals sure did clean up nice!

After Emma's brother dropped us off at school, we headed inside to the gymnasium. The place had been given a complete makeover. A giant banner with the words "NEON

NIGHTS" scrawled across welcomed us as we walked in. Festive bunches of balloons were scattered around the edges of the room, and the walls were draped with glow-in-the-dark posters. Black spotlights made the white and neon colors glow. To add to the effect, everyone was wearing flashing necklaces and bracelets.

"Oh, look!" said Jessi. "They're giving those away." Jessi strode confidently toward the far wall, where a bunch of boys were jumping up and down to the pounding music. The three of us followed. After we got some glowing plastic jewelry, we headed to the snack table and munched cookies and sipped juice. We watched the dance floor, where groups of boys and girls gathered, completely separated. Every once in a while one of the boys would hurl himself into a circle of girls, before laughing and rushing out again. His friends would cheer for him and slap his back enthusiastically when he rejoined them.

The music was getting really good, and Emma, Jessi, and I just had to dance. A bunch of the Kangaroos joined us on the dance floor: Brianna, Sarah, and Anna. Even two of the eighth graders, Grace and Anjali, danced with us for a little while. They both seemed really nice. It was a shame Mirabelle seemed determined to keep the team separated by grades. But at least we were getting a chance to hang out now!

At first Zoe wouldn't move, even though we dragged her onto the floor and bumped hips with her. But our enthusiasm was contagious, and we eventually wore her down. She started bobbing around a little bit. Many songs later my hair was stuck to my forehead in sweaty clumps.

But then, suddenly, the music changed, going from upbeat dance music to a slow song. Everyone froze.

Someone tapped me on the shoulder, startling me. It was Steven. Was he going to ask me to dance?

"Hey, um, my friend Matt wants to know if Zoe will dance with him," he said. "Can you ask?" Ah, I guessed not.

I walked over to Zoe, who had been watching the whole exchange. Before I could even ask her, she shook her head.

"You don't want to dance with Matt?" I asked.

"No, thanks," Zoe said. "I have to go to the bathroom."

"Sorry," I said to Steven, not really needing to translate. "I guess she doesn't want to."

Emma stepped in. "Hey, Steven, I'll dance with Matt." Leave it to Emma to know what to do. "And Devin will dance with you." *Wait, what?* I threw a dirty look at Emma.

"You w-will?" Steven stammered, his eyebrows shooting up in surprise.

I could have killed Emma. Sucking it up, I smiled at Steven and said, "Sure." The three of us walked out onto the dance floor, where Matt materialized. Steven put his arms around my waist, and I draped my arms loosely over his shoulders. It was incredibly awkward. I hardly knew Steven!

Luckily, I spotted Jessi, who appeared next to us, dancing with Cody. Had Jessi asked Cody to dance? Wondering about that proved a good distraction, because it gave me a break from thinking about if my palms were sweaty or if my breath smelled. She gave me a thumbs-up, then mouthed something I couldn't make out. I gave her a quizzical look, and she mouthed the words again: "He. Asked. Me."

Cody had asked Jessi to dance! I gave her a big smile and a wink. When the song was over, Emma came rushing over and cut between me and Steven. "Matt told me there's a photo booth! We gotta go!" I gave Steven a small smile, and he waved as he walked off. I looked over to Jessi, who kept dancing with Cody as a new song began to play.

"Jessi, we're going out into the hall," I called to her. "Come take pictures with us!"

Jessi excused herself from Cody and followed Emma and me. We grabbed Zoe on our way to the hallway, where a real old-fashioned photo booth had been set up.

Ahead of us in line a group of eighth graders was hogging the booth. Mirabelle was there, and so were a couple of the cool eighth graders from my algebra class. The whole group kept taking photos and cutting right back in for more.

"Hello, people are waiting," Emma said. We were missing the dance, waiting for them to finish up.

"Winners can take as many photos as we want." I recognized Trey Bishop, the eighth-grade captain of the boys' soccer team, from the pep rally. He poked a finger at us. "You losers have to wait."

A couple of the eighth graders started to crack up.

"So what? You're good at soccer. Big whoop." Emma wasn't intimidated at all. "Get back in line," she shot back.

"You guys shouldn't even be called 'Kangaroos.' You're a total embarrassment to the school," Trey said.

"At least we don't have to make fun of other people to feel good about ourselves," I said angrily. If I could stand up to Mirabelle, I certainly could tell this bully off. Everyone behind us was gathering around to see what was going on.

"At least we don't score on our own team." Huge laughter, much louder this time. I noticed Mirabelle was laughing too. I felt my blood start to boil.

I guess seeing Mirabelle laughing put Zoe over the edge too. She pushed her way to stand next to Emma.

"Stop being jerks!" she yelled.

That did it. That finally shut everyone up.

But then the boys just started laughing harder. Mirabelle didn't even try to hide her laughter. Some captain she was.

Stepping aside, Trey swept his arm out and motioned for us to use the photo booth. "Go right ahead," he said, still laughing. "Take some pictures. Just give me a copy so I can show everyone what losers look like."

As they walked away from the booth, they singsonged, "Losers, losers, losers." Mirabelle followed them back into the gymnasium, laughing all the way. *Traitor.*

Our good mood was entirely ruined. We didn't even feel like taking photos after that.

It felt like the Kangaroos had lost again, this time off

the field. And as if Mirabelle had never been a true teammate, now she was acting like an outright enemy. That
was no way for a team captain to act. I felt my eyes nar-
row. As the co-captain, it was up to me to do something.
Mirabelle and I were going to have a little chat at practice
on Monday. And this time I was looking forward to it.

CHAPTER TWELVE

That Sunday I told Kara over the phone all about what had happened at the dance.

"I can't believe she just walked away and didn't even stick up for you guys!" Kara said. "Well, maybe after everything you've told me about her, I can believe it. And her being a co-captain. It's just horrible!"

"The team can't keep going on like this. If Mirabelle can't be a good leader, I guess it's up to me," I said.

"You can do it, Devin!" Kara said. "The Cosmos—you know what it's like—we have a lot of team events, and the captains organize them. That's part of our job. Last week it was a frozen-yogurt social. Another time we had a Saturday pizza party. How do you guys do team bonding?"

That was easy to answer: We didn't.

Kara had some good ideas. So far the Kicks had had

only lame practices and games that we couldn't win. We should totally do something as a team. But there was just one thing. "I'm not sure Mirabelle would go for it, especially after what she did at the dance."

Kara's voice got stern and firm. "If she's awful to you, you can always talk to your coach. Mirabelle has got to be stopped. Maybe she shouldn't be co-captain anymore."

I shuddered. I had stood up to Mirabelle once, but thinking of telling her she shouldn't be captain anymore sent a chill up my spine. Speaking to Kara, however, gave me courage. "You're right," I said. "I'll talk to Coach if Mirabelle won't help. But I'm not sure if Coach will listen. Even though she used to be serious about soccer in college, she treats us like we're kindergartners. We don't get a chance to improve and work on our skills."

"That's so weird to me," said Kara. It was nice to get an outsider's perspective. It made me realize just how odd it actually was, having such a coddling coach. "Maybe if you told her how you felt?"

"I'll tackle Mirabelle first," I said. "Not literally, but maybe if she won't listen to reason, I'll have to resort to it!"

Kara laughed. "You can do it, Devin," she said encouragingly.

My best friend was right. The Kangaroos needed to bond as a team. And Mirabelle's laughing at us at the dance hadn't helped at all. She'd crossed the line.

I was ready to have it out with her and bring the team together.

All day Monday I kept practicing what I would say to Mirabelle that afternoon at practice.

Resolved, I headed into the locker room after school to change, ready to face Mirabelle. I was surprised at how empty and quiet it was, even though bags were strewn around and locker doors were halfway open. Then I noticed there was a commotion coming from the bathroom.

"What's going on?" I called out, heading to the back.

Opening the door, I found the whole team crowded inside. They stepped aside so I could see. There, on the mirror, scrawled in lipstick was a message for us. *BYE, LOSERS!* it said, with a big flourishing *M* at the bottom.

There was only one person who could possibly have done this.

"Mirabelle? She quit?" I couldn't believe it. I had been all ready to have it out with her, and she'd left the team?

"Not even," Emma said. "She transferred."

"What?" I asked, surprised.

From behind me Coach Flores said, "To Pinewood."

The faces of the girls around me dropped in shock.

"That is just perfect," Frida blurted out, laughing to herself. "Pinewood! I don't even know what to call that. Irony? Poetic justice? A made-for-TV movie?"

Coach Flores grabbed some paper towels and started to

furiously wipe Mirabelle's message off the mirror. It was the first time any of us had seen her angry. "Don't let this message discourage you. You girls are *not* losers. No way! It doesn't matter if we win or lose our games," she said as she continued to scrub. Leave it to Mirabelle to use a long-lasting lipstick. "I'm sure Mirabelle had her personal reasons for leaving. They probably didn't have anything to do with our team."

"Did she tell you that?" I asked.

"Well, I didn't talk to her directly," Coach admitted. "I received an e-mail from her dad."

"Did it say anything about how Mirabelle was transferring to go to a better team?" I wondered.

"No, nothing like that." Coach Flores stopped scrubbing at the mirror and turned around to face us. "Her dad just thanked me for being her coach and said that Mirabelle had been accepted to Pinewood on scholarship. Pinewood's a very good school. It's got excellent academic and athletic programs."

Jessi and I exchanged knowing glances.

"Aha!" I said. "So that's why she was so concerned about doing her best at the Pinewood game. She was up for a scholarship."

"And she knew they'd be watching her," Jessi said, and nodded in agreement.

It all made sense now. Mirabelle's insistence on making the lineup. Her saying she "needed" to win. Well, good for her. She'd gotten what she wanted.

"And I guess that's why she laughed at us at the dance, when the guys were calling us losers," I said. "Because she figured she'd never have to see us again."

"Well, we *will* see her again. We're playing Pinewood again in two weeks," Coach Flores said, frowning. "Wait— What? Who was calling you losers?"

We all exchanged worried glances. The guys on the soccer team were total jerks, but we didn't want to rat them out.

"Nobody," I said quickly. "It's fine."

Coach raised her eyebrows, but I could tell she was going to let the matter drop—at least for now.

"Look," she said. "I can see that nobody's in the mood to practice today. We can cancel. This is all a lot to take in. I'll be in my office if anyone needs me or wants to talk. Don't let this get you down, girls." She gave us a cheerful smile before heading to her office. The other girls walked back to their lockers to pack up, leaving me, Jessi, Emma, and Zoe alone.

"What did Coach mean when she said we're playing Pinewood again in two weeks?" I asked.

"There aren't enough teams in the league to fill the season, so we play some teams twice," Emma explained. "I think they do it by lottery or something."

"And we ended up with Pinewood again? I'd call that *losing* the lottery," I said.

"Me too," Jessi agreed. "Hey, since we're not practicing today, I'm gonna go watch Cody practice," Jessi announced.

I raised my eyebrows at her.

"You are?" I asked. "Maybe you should take the opportunity to catch up on homework instead?"

Jessi rolled her eyes. "Don't worry about it, *Mom*," she said sarcastically. "Cody invited me, at the dance on Friday. He said I should come watch him play sometime. Anyone else want to come?" She gave me a sly smile. "I bet Steven will be there."

"Ew, after what his teammates said to us at the dance?" Emma said. "No way am I gonna watch those jerks practice! Zoe and I are going shopping. Devin?"

I didn't feel like shopping, and I certainly didn't want to see the boys' soccer team either. Not after what they'd done. "It's okay. You guys go."

I knew what I had to do. It was way more important than shopping or helping Jessi drool over her crush. I had to get the Kangaroos together as a team. I couldn't talk to Mirabelle like I had planned, but it was time to let Coach Flores know exactly what I was thinking.

After the rest of the team left, I marched over to Coach Flores's office. She was sitting there, tilted way back in her chair, looking at her computer screen.

I knocked loudly on her door. "Can I come in?"

"Devin," Coach said, easing out of her seat. "How are you doing?" She motioned me in while opening a folding chair for me to sit on.

Coach reached into a drawer and pulled out a half-empty package of Girl Scout cookies. She removed the cookie tray from the box and offered me some with her usual smile. "I know this is hard," she said, "having a teammate leave in the middle of the season like this."

I nodded but didn't say anything. It was harder to speak my mind to Coach than I'd thought it would be. I'd rather face an angry Mirabelle. At least I didn't have to worry about hurting her feelings!

"What's bothering you, Devin?" she asked.

"Mirabelle always complained to me about how bad we were, and how we kept losing." I felt the words rush out of me. "Do *you* care that we're losers?"

"You girls are *not* losers. Don't say that. You're still in middle school. Sports should be for fun. Isn't that what I always say?"

"I'm not having fun," I said. "I don't think anybody is."

"Is that true?" Coach said. She looked surprised, and genuinely concerned.

I nodded. "Our team isn't very . . ." I searched around for the right word. "Cohesive. My friend back home, Kara, she's co-captain of her soccer team, and she said they do a lot of team-bonding stuff. After school, and even on the weekends. Why don't we do any of that?" I asked her.

"I didn't know you girls wanted to do that kind of thing. I just never want to take up all your time with soccer. I know you girls have lives outside of school. Trust me, I've been there before," Coach said wistfully.

"You played soccer, right?" I asked. "Mirabelle told me that."

"I did play once," she said, reaching into her desk and pulling out a framed newspaper article.

The article was titled THESE GIRLS CAN KICK: KENTVILLE KANGAROOS STATE CHAMPS TWO YEARS IN A ROW and featured a large photo of a team of smiling girls, wearing the blue-and-white Kentville uniform. Some of the girls were holding their pointer fingers up in the air in the *Number one* sign. Two girls in the front row held a large golden trophy between them, with 1992 STATE CHAMPIONS emblazoned across the front.

"Did you go to Kentville?" I asked.

"Yes." She nodded. "That's me." She pointed to one of the girls holding the trophy. I barely recognized her. She looked so young!

I quickly scanned the top of the article. *Maria Luisa Flores leads the Kentville Kangaroos to their second state win. The Kicks, as they are known to their fans for the arsenal of kicks they use against their opponents on the field, didn't disappoint. Just a little more than five minutes into the game, co-captain midfielder Flores landed a pass of forty yards to midfielder Kerry Coles . . .*

What? I shook my head in disbelief. The Kangaroos used to be good. In fact, they used to be great—state champions, even!

"You were on the team when it got its nickname?" I asked, still in shock. "Jessi and Emma said nobody even remembers where the name 'the Kicks' came from."

"Our coach drilled us nonstop on kicks—push, instep,

outside, toe, heel, you name it," Coach Flores said. "We had a kick for every and any situation. And since we were the Kangaroos, too, our fans started calling us 'the Kicks.'"

She got a faraway look in her eye. "When I was your age, all I did was play soccer. Nothing else. My parents made me practice every day so I could get a college scholarship. Which I did." She paused for emphasis. "But I ended up hating it."

"Why?" I asked.

"There was too much pressure," she said. "All the fun had been taken out of it for me. It was all about winning, not about having a good time."

"Then why are you a soccer coach, if you hate it?" I asked.

"I loved the game. I just hated the pressure and not being able to pursue other interests I had," she said. "I'm a soccer coach because I don't want kids to go through what I went through. All that yelling and screaming. Trust me, you don't want that."

"You're right," I said. "That doesn't sound fun at all. But can't there be something in the middle?" I suggested.

"What do you mean?" she said.

"We *want* to win," I replied immediately. Mirabelle thought we were losers. We had to prove her wrong.

"But, Devin," she said, "winning isn't everything."

"I know that," I said. "But feeling like we don't have a shot at being any good—that's worse. Can you help us at least try to get better?"

Coach Flores sat up straight in her chair, looking at me curiously. "Does this have anything to do with what you said in the locker room, about someone calling you losers?"

"It's part of it," I admitted. "We want to do better as a team. And we don't want to be the laughingstocks of the school. There is *nothing* fun about that!"

"What? Laughingstocks?" Coach looked upset. "Out with it, Devin. I need to know what's going on."

I sighed. I knew she wasn't going to let it rest, so I quickly told her what had happened.

"For the record, I want to make it clear that Steven and Cody had nothing to do with it," I said. They were both nice guys. "And please don't go to Coach Valentine. The boys will just come after us even more," I pleaded.

Coach had a pained look on her face. "I had no idea," she said. "Now, don't worry about the boys' team. I promise they won't bother you again. And if the girls' team really wants to try to win, I'll do my best. But I'm not going to force you girls to do anything."

"But what if we want you to tell us what to do?" I said. "We want your guidance. We need a leader. Mirabelle— she might have been a good player, but she wasn't a good leader. She was more of a bully than anything else."

Coach sighed. "I am so sorry you felt that way," she said. "I always got a funny vibe from that girl, like maybe she wasn't who she was pretending to be when she was talking to me."

Coach had caught on more than I'd realized. "Yeah," I said. "She wasn't always very nice." That was an understatement.

Coach shook her head. "I'm sorry you had to deal with that, as her co-captain," she said. "How can I help lead you girls? How can I give you what you need to have fun out there?"

I saw a spark in Coach's eyes I had never seen before. At the very least I had gotten her thinking a little differently. I talked to her about my ideas for team-bonding events, and for some drills we could run. Coach began to get excited and began to come up with a lot of great ideas. She knew a ton about formations, and she had done lots of different kinds of drills in her heyday. By the time our practice would have been over, and my dad was outside waiting to pick me up, we both felt energized and excited about the possibilities.

"Thanks for coming to talk to me, Devin," she said. "I know it must have been hard for you, but I had no idea any of you were feeling like this or that the team was being teased. I'll make sure to let you all know that we have an open dialogue here. I just want you girls to be happy, and I mistakenly thought what *I* would have wanted at your age is what *you* girls wanted too. I'm sorry about that."

Coach Flores was supernice. If she could put her ideas into action and start to lead the team, she could be the best coach ever! "It's okay," I told her. "I'm just excited for our next practice now!"

Coach smiled. "You know what? So am I! See you tomorrow!" she said.

"You got it, Coach!" I raced out of her office, feeling like the weight of the world had been lifted off my shoulders. No more Mirabelle. And Coach was open to all my ideas! I felt like singing as I climbed into the car.

"Wow!" Dad remarked as he looked at my face. "You're all smiles!"

I felt my grin widen. "I have a feeling that the Kangaroos have just turned over a new leaf!"

CHAPTER THIRTEEN

I could barely sleep that night, I was so charged about all the new plans for the Kangaroos.

But there were some problems I wasn't sure even Coach could help with. Like Emma's clumsiness, Frida's not wanting to be on the team at all, and Zoe's stage fright. A lightbulb went off in my head. I didn't know what to do about Emma just yet, but I think I had a way to help Zoe and Frida!

When I got up in the morning, I grabbed my phone and sent a group text to Jessi, Emma, Zoe, Frida, Brianna, Sarah, and Anna.

New day, new Kangaroos! Meet me after practice. I have an idea.

I raced to our dusty practice field after school. Even the crummy garbage-can goals looked better to me today. This was a new start! But I could tell the rest of the team didn't feel so happy, especially the eighth graders.

I overheard two eighth graders, Grace and Anjali, talking. They were the girls who'd hung out with us for a little bit at the dance. I didn't know them too well, but they seemed pretty nice.

"We were supposed to be friends," Anjali was complaining. "She didn't even say good-bye."

Part of the problem with our team was that the seventh graders and eighth graders didn't interact much. That had been mostly Mirabelle's doing. But now that she was out of the picture, it was time to change that.

Coach Flores wasn't there yet, but I took charge.

"Gather round!" I yelled. Some of them looked surprised to hear me raising my voice.

When everyone had gotten together, I started talking. "Look," I said. "I know things haven't been so great. But we can turn it around. I found out yesterday that back in the nineties the Kicks were state champions two years in a row! In fact, that's when they got their nickname. It was because of their awesome footwork. And Coach Flores was on the championship team! "

It sounded like a group of bees had descended on the field. Everyone started buzzing at the news!

"If we were state champions once, we can be again!" I yelled over the girls' excited chatter. "It's time to turn this team around and be a team worthy of the name 'Kicks.' With Mirabelle gone I need an eighth grader to be co-captain with me. Any nominations?"

An eighth grader with curly blond hair, named Giselle, stepped forward.

"I nominate Grace," she said. Quietly under her breath she added, "That's who I wanted the first time around."

Anjali chimed in right away. "I second it!"

I looked around the group. "Is that okay with everyone?" Everyone nodded.

"Grace is the new eighth-grade captain," I said. "I'll let Coach know we all agreed on it." A few people started cheering, while Grace smiled shyly. I could feel the atmosphere begin to lighten, and then suddenly we all heard a funny humming noise.

When we turned to look, we saw Coach Flores coming onto the field, two bags slung over her shoulders—a big one and a small one.

The sound appeared to be coming from a new whistle she kept blowing into every few seconds. It sounded silly, like something from a cartoon. We couldn't help but crack up.

"*What is* that thing?" Emma asked, laughing.

Coach Flores dropped the bags and then held up the whistle with one hand. It was plastic, red, and shaped like a tiny submarine. "It's a kazoo."

"I knew that," Frida said as Coach Flores passed the kazoo around. When Emma got her hands on it, she immediately tried it out and blew into the wrong end. A wimpy whine dribbled out.

"Try humming into it, not blowing," Coach suggested.

Something about her was way different. I couldn't put my finger on it, but she had a gleam in her eyes that she hadn't had before. Even with a silly kazoo it looked like this Coach Flores meant business.

"It's been brought to my attention that you guys have felt like you haven't been learning many new skills at practice," Coach Flores said.

The girls looked around at one another quizzically. It was true. *But how did Coach Flores know that?* their faces asked.

"So we're going to try to do things differently today," she said, her eyes sparkling. "And the activities won't have anything to do with soccer."

She turned over the big bag, and a bunch of balls came bouncing out. There were rubber bouncy balls, tennis balls, volleyballs, a basketball, and even some footballs. We all looked around at one another, totally confused.

"You'll never guess what I have in here," Coach said as she pulled open the smaller bag. She started to pull out a bunch of long socks! There was an excited energy in the air. What was all this stuff for? Did this have something to do with our sock swap?

"Now, which game do you want to play? The one with the balls or with the socks?" Coach asked us, smiling that familiar smile of hers.

In a unanimous vote we all raised our hands for the socks. Coach laughed. "Okay, this game is for teams of two. Split yourselves into pairs." While Coach still seemed as nice as ever, there was something more forceful about her too.

"Hey, sock buddy," Jessi said to me. "Let's be a team."

Coach gave us directions while handing out a single sock to each pair. "One of you has to wear this as a blindfold."

Jessi wrinkled her nose. "I hope they're clean," she joked.

"Don't worry. They're brand-new," Coach said, and laughed. Then she rolled the rest of the socks up into individual balls and put them in piles around the field. "Now here's what we're going to do. The person not wearing the blindfold will be the driver. The one wearing the blindfold will be the tank. The driver will direct the tank by giving her verbal directions. The object of the game is to work together to grab a sock from the pile. Once you grab a sock, your team can eliminate another team when your tank hits another tank with a balled-up sock. Last team standing wins. Got it?"

It sounded a bit confusing, and totally ridiculous, but more important, it sounded like fun.

"I should be the tank," Jessi said. "You'll be way better at giving directions."

I agreed. I wrapped the sock blindfold around Jessi's head.

"If only Cody could see you now," I joked. Jessi laughed as I took her hand and led her to the starting position.

We gathered in a circle around the randomly placed piles of socks. Coach blew her kazoo, and we were off!

Jessi immediately lurched forward way too fast, putting herself right into Emma's path.

Zoe yelled, "Emma, turn right, right!" Of course, blindfolded Emma was twice as disoriented as usual, so she moved left and bumped right into Jessi. I was doubled over laughing already.

"Devin, where do I go?" Jessi said, her hands in front of her like a zombie. She shuffled slowly toward what she thought was the middle.

I tried hard to stop laughing, barely gasping out, "Forty-five degrees left, take five big steps, and there's a sock on the ground right there."

We were a good team. Jessi found the sock. Right behind her was Frida, moving superslowly with her blindfold on. Sarah was trying to get her to move faster.

"Now flip around a hundred and eighty degrees!" I yelled at Jessi. All the drivers were yelling at the same time. It was so noisy, it was hard for the tanks to hear their drivers.

Once I saw that Jessi had turned the right way around, I screamed loudly, "Aim, and FIRE!" Jessi didn't hesitate. She threw her sock directly in front of her, and it bounced off Frida's arm.

"Got 'em!" I cried, jumping up and down in celebration.

Right then a sock dropped out of the sky, looping toward Jessi's head. "Duck, Jessi, duck!" I yelled. Again she did exactly as I said, and the sock missed her.

It took another ten minutes, but Jessi and I won by out-maneuvering Grace and Anjali to become the last team standing. I ran over to Jessi as she ripped her blindfold off, my adrenaline pumping so hard, I leaped right into her arms for a big hug.

"Want to play again?" Coach Flores asked with a grin. Of course we did!

"Switch partners!" Coach tooted into her kazoo. The rest of practice zoomed by as we took turns being tanks and drivers with different partners. I didn't win again, maybe because I wasn't partners with Jessi, but it was still superfun. Everyone was laughing at the end when Coach gathered us together.

"So what did you learn from this game?" Coach asked.

"You gotta listen to your driver!" Jessi said.

"When you're a tank, you gotta trust your driver first?" Frida chimed in.

"Be patient with your tank," Emma added. "Especially me."

"You are all correct!" Coach Flores said. "Listening, trusting your teammates, and patience are all incredibly important tools! But my favorite lesson that this game teaches is that, sometimes, it's important to just let loose and have fun."

Coach was a genius! Not only had this silly game helped our teamwork skills, but our team had never laughed so much together. And she'd still done it her way—the fun way!

I caught Coach Flores's eye, and she gave me a wink. She was right: Listening *was* an important skill. And she had clearly taken my words to heart. I couldn't wait to see what else she had in store for us! But first I had my own plan to put into action—turning Zoe and Frida into two of the Kicks' most valuable players!

CHAPTER FOURTEEN

While the rest of our teammates headed to the locker room, Jessi, Emma, Zoe, Frida, Brianna, Sarah, Anna, and I stayed behind. They were still smiling over the great practice when they huddled around me.

"That was so much fun!" Anna cried, her big brown eyes shining.

Brianna nodded. "I'm so busy with all my other extra-curricular activities, I was thinking of dropping soccer. But not anymore!"

Zoe looked at me curiously. "Did you have anything to do with this, Devin? I saw you going into Coach's office yesterday."

I smiled. "Yes, and that's when I found out about the Kicks being state champs!"

"Well, whatever you said worked," Emma said. "That was awesome! I feel like we really have a chance at being a team now. Maybe a champion team. Who knows? Maybe history will repeat itself."

"So what's your big idea?" Jessi asked, her eyebrow raised.

"Yeah, we've been wondering all day," Frida added. "I told my mom I would be late coming home from practice today. She was shocked! I'm usually texting her the second it's over to come and get me."

I took a deep breath. I hadn't thought this all the way through, but the glimmer of an idea had taken hold in my mind last night. I had to give it a try.

"Frida," I began, "I know your mom is making you play soccer, but Jessi said you're a really great player when you're paying attention."

"It's not like I hate soccer or anything," Frida admitted. "It's just that I'd rather be acting."

"Well, what if you could practice your acting and play soccer at the same time?" I asked hopefully.

Everyone looked at me, surprised.

"Um, how exactly would she do that?" Sarah wondered.

"What if we could give you a part to play at every game?" I said. I had my fingers crossed that Frida would be willing to give this a try. "Like, maybe one week you could be an undercover spy, sent to infiltrate our soccer team? Or you could be a secret princess who just wants to live a normal life and play soccer and stuff?"

I looked eagerly at Frida. Her hand was on her chin, rubbing it slightly as she thought.

"Hmmmm," she said. "Interesting. So I could play soccer, but I'd really be acting?"

I nodded. "Each week we would give you a new character with different motivations, so you'd get to try different roles while you played."

Slowly a smile spread across Frida's face. "Devin, that's brilliant! I can't believe I never thought of that before."

Jessi jumped in. "But all the characters will be good players who want to win, right?"

I laughed. "Of course!"

"So is that the only reason you asked us here?" Sarah asked.

"No." I shook my head. "I was hoping there would be a way for Frida to help Zoe."

"Me?" Zoe asked, her eyes growing wide.

"You get stage fright," I explained. "Frida has no problem getting onstage in front of a crowd of people. She's got to have some tips."

Frida smiled. "You bet I do! Did you know that three quarters of all performers get stage fright? It happens to everyone—even to me sometimes! Sure, there are some tricks that could work for Zoe when she's playing soccer."

"So why don't you talk to Zoe?" I suggested. "Then we can take turns playing with her, while some of us sit and pretend to be the audience."

Frida grabbed Zoe enthusiastically. "This is going to be great! First you've got to visualize the game going perfectly. If you picture it going well, it will! Another proven winner is to picture everyone in the crowd as one person. Picture everyone as Emma, or your mom, or even your pet! Whoever your biggest cheerleader is."

They walked off together, Zoe taking in every word Frida was saying.

Jessi playfully tapped me on the shoulder. "I've got to hand it to you, Captain. That was some smart thinking."

After Zoe and Frida huddled for a while, we took turns playing with Zoe and being the audience. She really started to loosen up, and soon she was zipping all over the field. My jaw dropped.

"See? We told you she was good," Emma said with a smile.

I remembered back to the sleepover at Emma's when we had wished on the shooting star. I think my wish was starting to come true!

I gulped. I was sitting between Frida and Emma, a spoon in my hand. Would the Kangaroos be able to overcome their toughest challenge yet?

We were all sitting together that Thursday night in the Sock Hop, a fun restaurant decorated to look like a 1950s diner. The waitresses wore poodle skirts and saddle shoes, while the waiters were dressed all in white, wearing bow ties and little white paper hats. The floor was black-and-white tiles, and every wall inside was filled with old posters and advertisements, like the one offering soda for two cents a can.

The Kangaroos had taken over a long white and steel table in the back, with bright red vinyl chairs. Our parents and Coach Flores were there, getting ready to take photos of the action. My dad had his trusty video camera in his hand. He gave me a thumbs-up as he smiled. I looked at the door hopefully. The only thing missing was Jessi. I had texted her earlier but had gotten no answer, which was weird. But the Giant Purple People Eater, a massive ice-cream sundae, was about to come for us.

Our waitress, who had her red hair teased up into a puffy hairdo, smiled. "Are you girls ready?" she asked.

"Yes!" we yelled in unison, pounding the table with our fists. A gong went off in the back, temporarily drowning out our voices. Then two more servers emerged, each carrying a huge wooden bucket.

Inside each bucket were twenty scoops of amazing ice cream of all flavors.

That's right, we had ordered *two* Giant Purple People Eaters. The sign at the Sock Hop said that this sundae would eat you before you could eat it! And we were going to race to see which team could finish theirs first.

Emma, an ice-cream junkie, had always wanted to try this and had talked the rest of us into it as a team-building exercise. Every person to finish a Giant Purple People Eater got their name on a plaque on the wall. The manager of the Sock Hop had agreed to put the Kangaroos' name up on the wall if we could eat two of them in less than ten minutes. At first Coach Flores had said no way, that part of being on a sports team was learning good nutrition. And my mom was horrified when I told her! But we wore Coach down, and I was able to talk my mom into letting me do it, with a little help from my dad. It was all in good fun! And I had a feeling once would be enough. This definitely wouldn't become part of our daily diets.

The oversize buckets were so big, we had to stand up over them. This was going to be disgusting. We all exchanged worried glances.

"It's gigantic," Zoe said, cringing.

"I'll eat your share, don't worry," Emma said, practically drooling at the sight of all that ice cream.

Our waitress hit a switch on the jukebox, and the song "Purple People Eater" began to play. It was a silly song from the 1950s.

"Go!" she yelled.

We dove in, and stuffed our faces with ice cream as fast as we could while the music played loudly and our parents cheered us on.

Halfway through our bucket, I stopped and took a few deep breaths. I was running out of room in my stomach.

"Keep going!" Emma said, her mouth crammed with ice cream. She had it smeared all over her face.

Less than ten minutes later, we'd done it. We'd finished forty scoops of ice cream. Our waitress banged the gong five times to sound our success. Everyone in the diner cheered for us. We all high-fived one another, even though our hands were pretty sticky.

"I think I'm going to be sick," Emma moaned. "Whose stupid idea was this, anyway?"

Even Brianna's long blond hair had ice cream in it. "It was yours, you nut!" she reminded Emma.

"Ugh," said Zoe. "Nuts sound disgusting."

It was too much. We were all laughing our heads off, which only made our stomachs hurt more.

"You girls," our waitress said, laughing. "You're a hoot—a real bunch of kicks!"

"That's because we *are* the Kicks!" Grace, our new eighth-grade captain said, with a messy ice-cream-smeared smile.

"Kicks, Kicks, Kicks, Kicks," Anna started chanting. Soon everyone joined in, even our parents.

I looked around the room, at everyone smiling and laughing. We were more a team than we'd ever been before. But I couldn't be completely happy. Where was Jessi?

CHAPTER FIFTEEN

Later that night, after recovering from a massive brain freeze and a bit of a stomachache, I called Jessi's house, half-expecting her not to be there.

"Hello?" She picked up.

"Where were you tonight?" I asked, launching in before she could say anything else. "Are you okay? Are you sick? I texted you, like, five times. I was getting worried!"

There was a pause on her end. "Devin, I couldn't go because I couldn't go," she said. Then I heard a small sniffle from her end of the phone.

"Jessi, what's wrong?" I asked.

"I didn't text you back because my cell got taken away. And I'm off the team. I can't play soccer anymore! I'm flunking math and Spanish, and my mom said the rest of my report card is almost as bad."

I was too stunned to speak. I knew Jessi wasn't doing

great in school, but I'd had no idea she was failing. "You can't even go to practice or team events?" I finally managed to ask.

"Nothing. It's straight to school and then straight back. That's it."

"I'm so sorry." I didn't know what else to say. This was crushing news. Not just for Jessi but for all of us. We had just started to come together as a team, and now we were losing one of our best players.

"My parents say I can start playing if I get my grades up," Jessi said.

"Let me know if I can help," I said.

Jessi gave a little hiccup. I could tell she was holding back tears. "I can't believe how bad I messed up," she said sadly.

"Don't worry. If you work hard and stay focused, you'll get those grades up!" I tried to encourage her.

I heard Mrs. Dukes's voice in the background.

"I have to go,"Jessi said in a very tiny, un-Jessi-like voice. "Bye, Devin."

"Bye." I put the phone down. I felt so bad for Jessi!

I didn't know how to help Jessi, but I knew I had to do something for the team. We really had a lot of momentum behind us now. Losing Jessi could totally derail us.

So I found Zoe the next day during lunch and explained the situation to her. "We need you to score. Do you think you're up to it?"

Zoe nodded slowly. "Frida and I have been getting

together every day. She's really giving me some great tips. I'm pretty sure they're working. I really won't know, though, until we have a real game." She started to get a little pale. "But I'll do my best."

"No pressure, but we have our rematch with Pinewood coming up. I really don't want to lose to them again. *Especially* now that Mirabelle's on their team."

I saw a spark in Zoe's eye as I mentioned our former teammate. "Beating them, that would be sweet," Zoe said.

I really hoped she'd be able to get over her fear of playing under pressure. The team needed her now more than ever.

Soccer practice would have been perfect the next Monday, except for the fact that Jessi wasn't there. Coach Flores had us running some pretty tough drills on the kicks that had given our team its nickname, but then we ended by playing a fun game of Capture the Flag with soccer balls. Coach's new style was really working. The fun stuff balanced out the hard work and kept us feeling like a team that was in this together.

"Great practice, Kicks," Coach told us, smiling.

Zoe, Emma, and I were feeling pretty good after practice and decided to head over to the local diner for a snack.

"I wish Jessi were here," Zoe said sadly.

Before Emma or I could say anything, we heard a shout. "Look out!"

A Frisbee appeared out of nowhere, heading right for

us. All three of us ducked, but the Frisbee still managed to crash into Emma.

"Ouch!" she said, rubbing her forehead.

"Sorry. Are you okay?" a boy said, running toward us. Emma nodded.

"Um, can I have my Frisbee back?" he asked. I picked up the Frisbee and tossed it back. Somehow, as if by magic, it curved back around and threatened to decapitate Emma again.

"Whoa, what're you doing?" Emma said, this time getting out of the way, barely.

"You should just always walk around with a helmet," Zoe said, and laughed.

"Sorry," I said to her while picking up the Frisbee and handing it directly over to its owner this time.

Poor Emma. She never failed to trip over something, and she could always be counted on to knock things over. *Wait a minute.* A brilliant thought hit me. If flying objects were magnetically attracted to Emma, which they obviously were, it made sense that soccer balls would be too. I bet Emma would be totally unfazed by soccer balls zooming at her. Maybe she'd be good at deflecting them too.

Instead of getting in the way, which she always did on the field, we could turn her weakness into a strength. *Emma as goalie!*

I got really excited. This would solve so many problems! For one, she would always be facing the right way, which would already make her twice as effective. She also wouldn't have to worry about being in position ever again. Huge plus. Most of all, goalies were *supposed* to get in the way, and nobody got in the way better than Emma.

On top of that, if Emma was goalie, she could swing her arms around all she wanted. In fact, that's what she was supposed to do.

As we sat down in a booth and ordered our food, I kept seeing Emma as the Kicks' goalie. By the time my grilled cheese had arrived, I was ready. I was certain my idea was genius. If I could get Emma to agree.

First a little test. I threw a fry at her.

Direct hit.

"Hey, what're you doing?" she said, launching her own fry in my direction. She missed, of course, the potato missile falling harmlessly a few feet away.

"I just wanted to get your attention." I couldn't stop a grin from spreading across my face. "There was something else I was wondering. Have you ever played goalie before?"

She shook her head. "Nope. Never really occurred to me, I guess."

"Maybe you should give it a try," I encouraged her. "I think you'd be a natural at it."

"If being goalie is so great, how come nobody ever wants to play goalie?" Emma asked.

"Well, most people don't understand that being goalie is actually a very rewarding role," I said, using my best sales pitch. "A goalie needs to be both mentally and physically strong. They need to be able to stay positive when they get scored on. And we need someone the team trusts in that position."

"Why would they trust me? I scored on our own team!" Emma reminded me.

"They trust you because you are always so positive and want everyone to do their best," I said. "Plus, if you're in the goal, you can't score on yourself!"

Zoe laughed at that, and Emma joined in.

"That's a good point," she said, before taking a bite of her hamburger and munching thoughtfully. "If you think I'll be good as a goalie, I'm willing to give it a try, Captain," she said once she had swallowed.

I smiled. The Kicks kept getting better and better!

"I got it, I got it!" Emma screamed when a Rancho Verdes Viper got close enough to take a shot. The shot was weak, but Emma dove a little late and the ball dribbled in for a score. 1–0. Even though she was a natural, it was taking some time to get Emma adjusted to goal. But it was only her first game—and an away game, at that.

"Shoot," she said, shaking her head.

Before we could even say anything to encourage her, Emma's enthusiasm bounced right back. "I'll stop the next one, no problem." She shifted back and forth on her heels and clapped her goalie gloves.

"Let's go, dee-fense!" It was Emma's first official time

in goal, and it looked like she was loving it. For one, she could certainly yell louder than just about anyone else. "You guys need to help me out; it's not just me against the world here!"

When Rancho Verdes threatened with another scoring chance, Emma snuffed it out by leaping into a pile of bodies and emerging with the ball. Now that she could use her hands, Emma was magic.

Our entire defense was so much better. The skills that Coach Flores had been teaching us had really helped. We had learned to actually communicate on the field. Led by Emma, directing traffic in front of her, our back line was looking great. Especially when Emma managed to stop the next three Rancho Verdes shots. Her entire family chanted her name after each save: "Em-ma!" Em-ma!" Soon all the Kangaroo parents were doing it.

There was no doubt about it: Emma was brilliant in goal. She had no problem being the last line of defense. It didn't even faze her. In fact, she liked it. Plus, deflecting the ball miraculously turned out to be a natural skill. If a ball could get past her, it probably deserved to go in.

"Frida, watch number ten!" Emma shouted.

"I got her," Frida hollered back. A motivated Frida was like a freight train. She had eagerly agreed to step out of the goal for Emma and move to midfield instead. For this game she was playing the part of a girl whose mother wanted her to become a dancer and forbid her to play soccer. She had to sneak out to get to practices and games.

It seemed crazy, but it was working! Frida with a part to play was more committed than I had ever seen her. She turned back another Viper attack with ease.

For offense we had Zoe, Brianna, Grace's friend Megan, and me. Coach Flores started Zoe, Megan, and me. Without Jessi and her speed to stretch the defense, the middle of the field was crowded. I wasn't good enough to dribble through multiple defenders—that was Mirabelle's specialty—but I could be enough of a threat to attract some attention. We still didn't know what Zoe would be able to do, but I was hopeful.

Before the game had begun, Frida had made Zoe drink some orange juice. "It lowers blood pressure and lessens anxiety," she'd explained. Then they'd gone over Zoe's positive visualization and deep breathing techniques. This game would be the real test to see if it worked.

Coach's strategy going into the second half of the game was something she called the "rope-a-dope." We weren't sure what that meant, but when she explained it to us, it made a lot of sense.

"They're crowding around the ball whenever we hold it for a while. Midfielders, try to keep it on one side of the field, so they get used to looking only that way." Rancho Verdes was disorganized on defense, just like we'd been a few weeks ago. Coach explained the rest of the plan to us. It was crazy, but it just might work!

When we got back out on the field, Grace and I did exactly what Coach wanted us to. We used short passes to keep the ball on the left side as much as possible. What we were hoping would be our secret weapon, Zoe, was stationed way across on the other side. Because she looked so small, so unthreatening, Rancho Verdes soon started ignoring her. Which was good for our game plan, and good for Zoe's nerves. The fewer people watching her the better!

Zoe just kept hanging out, sneaking up when she could. Finally, when she had so much space around her that it looked like she was on an island, I boomed a pass all the way over to her. Even then their defense was slow to recover, because, really, what reason did they have to be afraid of Zoe?

Their goalie wasn't ready when Zoe pulled up thirty yards away. I held my breath. Would Zoe freeze up? But she planted her foot and blasted a shot toward the goal. With nobody to get in the way, and their goalie totally unprepared, Zoe's shot zoomed right in. We were tied, 1–1! Not only had we scored but it looked like Zoe's soccer stage fright was cured!

Now that the Vipers knew how dangerous Zoe was, they overcompensated by concentrating on her. Meanwhile, the ball got passed up the field, making its way to right in front of me. With all the attention on Zoe, I had just one defender to beat, which was easy.

I made sure to follow through on my kick, and my shot caught the goalie flat-footed. It was my first goal as a Kangaroo! It was a huge moment for me. Plus now the score was 2–1, Kangaroos. *We were actually leading a game!* My family was going nuts up in the stands—especially my dad.

"Go, Devin!" he yelled, as Maisie jumped up and down with excitement.

With a few minutes left our defense stuttered a little, and Emma collided with Frida on a loose ball, which rolled on into the goal. Still, when the referee blew the whistle to stop the game, the score was 2–2.

"Tie game!" the referee declared.

I couldn't believe it. We hadn't lost! Zoe charged from across the field and leaped into my arms. I tried to catch her, but her forward momentum knocked us both onto the ground. Emma ran over to pick us up, and then we linked arms as we skipped all the way back to the Rancho Verdes visitors' locker room, cheering with our teammates all the way. The only bummer was that Jessi wasn't with us. I wished she could have been in on the action or at least seen us!

Inside, everyone pounded on the lockers, all of us giddy. Sure, it wasn't a win, but who cared? After five straight losses this tie was HUGE. After a few minutes of letting the racket continue, Coach shushed us.

"Great job today, Kangaroos," she said.

"But I've got a confession to make," Coach Flores continued, suddenly serious. "When we first started the season, I didn't know you cared this much. I figured we'd just kick a couple of balls around, spend some time outside, with no pressure whatsoever. I see now that you girls wanted more than that. And I hope that these last couple of weeks I've shown you that I'm here to help."

She looked over at me, giving me a wink. "I think it's safe to say that we all learned it's possible to play hard and still have fun, right?"

Everyone cheered. We got together for a group hug. "Kangaroos on three," Coach Flores said. "One, two, three!"

"Kangaroos!" we all cheered.

I don't know where this Coach Flores had been earlier in the season, but she was now one of the best coaches I'd ever had!

CHAPTER SIXTEEN

One thing was missing from all our success: Jessi. She had been off the team for a week now, and we knew she was miserable missing out on all the fun we'd been having lately. I had an idea to try to cheer her up at least a little bit. After the Rancho Verdes game, when my family came to congratulate me, my dad clutching his video camera, I asked him, "Can we put this game on YouTube?"

"Sure!" he said, beaming. This was the first time I had asked him to do that with a Kangaroo game. Let's face it, none of the previous games had been worth sharing!

Later that night, when the video was finally done uploading, I sent Jessi an e-mail with the link.

Missed you today! I wrote. *But guess what? We tied! Check it out!*

After practice on Wednesday, Emma, Zoe, and I decided

to stop by Jessi's house for a surprise visit. I called ahead to make sure it was okay with her mom.

"Hi, girls," Mrs. Dukes said, greeting us at the door quietly. "Come on in. Jessi's in her room. But don't stay too long. She's got to finish her homework."

"Sure thing, Mrs. Dukes," I said.

When we got to the door of her room, Jessi was on her bed, turned away from us, watching the YouTube video of our soccer game on her laptop.

"Hey, Jessi!" Emma exclaimed.

Surprised, Jessi screamed, slammed her computer lid down, and threw her laptop off her bed before shouting, "Homework! It's homework!" The three of us collapsed on the ground, rolling around in laughter.

"You should have seen your face," I said, trying to point at her while holding my sides.

"I thought you guys were my mom!"

After Jessi cleared clothes off her huge bed, we all squeezed onto the mattress together.

"I can't get over the video of the game," Jessi said, her eyes shining. "You guys were awesome. It's like you're a totally different team." Then she frowned. "And I'm not on it! At this rate I'm going to be grounded forever," she groaned. "My grades are so not getting better fast enough. You wouldn't believe how often my mom calls my teachers now. I swear she has Mrs. Clarke on speed dial."

Jessi picked up a tennis ball and threw it against the wall, over and over. "I'm gonna go crazy if I stay cooped up!"

Suddenly I got an idea.

"Hey," I said. "Did your mom get you a tutor to help you with math?"

Jessi shook her head. "No," she said. "We talked about it, but I haven't gotten one yet."

"Hang on a sec," I said. "I'll be right back."

Leaving the three of them behind and confused, I went down the hall to find Jessi's mom. I should have done this a lot earlier, but Jessi hadn't seem interested. Now I was sure she'd be all for my idea—especially if it meant getting her back on the Kicks! But I wanted to clear it with her mom first.

Jessi's mom was in the kitchen, cutting apples and pears into slices for us. I blurted out my plan.

"I'd love to be Jessi's math tutor," I said. "I know I can get her to concentrate. I'm in eighth-grade algebra. I don't want to sound like I'm bragging, but I'm really good at math."

Mrs. Dukes laughed. "Jessi, concentrate on studying? I've been trying to get that girl to do that for years!"

"Can we try it?" I said. "We can see how it goes. If it doesn't help, then we won't do it anymore. But if it does help, if her math teacher sees an improvement, maybe she can come back on the team? We really, really need her back in time for the Pinewood game," I pleaded.

"If you can get her grades up, we'll see what we can do about her being on the soccer team," Jessi's mom said.

"I'll tell you what. Mrs. Clarke said she has a big math test coming up in a week. If she does well on it, then she can play."

"No problem, Mrs. Dukes. We'll handle it!" I ran up the stairs two at a time to go tell Jessi what the deal was.

"Seriously? She said I can play if I get a good grade on my next math test?" Jessi was beyond excited. "I'd do anything to be on the team again!" She gave me a huge hug. "And I don't want to miss our rematch against Pinewood. I want to prove to Mirabelle that we're not losers!"

"We're doing so much better, but we can't win without you," Emma said. Zoe nodded in agreement.

I moved back a few steps and looked right into Jessi's eyes. "Jessi, you gotta step up! You actually have to study. No goofing off or procrastinating. Got it?"

Jessi stood up tall and gave me a mock salute. "Yes, sir!" she said.

CHAPTER SEVENTEEN

It was almost October, and the Pinewood game was only a week away. I couldn't believe how fast time had gone by, and how much things had changed since my first day at Kentville Middle School.

Kara and I still texted every day. When I woke up Monday morning, a text was waiting for me.

Ruffle cardigan, denim skirt! What r u wearing? Have a gr8 day!

I grinned as I looked at the photo of Kara's smiling face. I was so glad we were keeping our morning tradition, even though my look had changed. Mom had taken me shopping a few weeks before to revamp my wardrobe from Connecticut prep to California fresh. I threw on a polka-dotted cami in cobalt blue and a pair of skinny jeans, finished off, of course, with flip-flops! I had a pair in just about every color now. Today I wore my blue ones.

I raced out the door and hopped into the van, where my dad was waiting. Mom had driven Maisie to school, so we had some alone time to chat about the team.

"The only thing is, we need more fans to cheer us on at the Pinewood game," I told him. "When we went to Pinewood, their entire stands were filled with people in purple and yellow. It was pretty intimidating. I want the Panthers to feel the same way when they come here, especially Mirabelle."

"You know you can count on me, your mom, and Maisie to be there cheering you on," my dad said.

"I know," I said. "But we need an extra boost of people, not just our families. We need all of Kentville Middle School behind us to give us a true home-field advantage!"

"Devin, after seeing how you took on the role of leader with the Kangaroos, I know there is nothing you can't do if you put your mind to it," my dad said as he pulled up to the school.

As I went to meet Jessi at the library during lunch later that day, I tried to think of some ways to fill the stands. I had started tutoring Jessi over the weekend, and she was already showing a lot of improvement. I had my fingers crossed that she'd rock her math test! It was in only two days. If she did well, her mom would let her back on the team! When I got to the library, Jessi was waiting, eager to get started.

"Practice test?" she asked excitedly.

I had to laugh. This was a different Jessi. All it took

was some strong motivation, and all her crazy Jessi energy became concentrated on her schoolwork like a laser beam. If she kept it up, she could join Brianna in the 4.0 club!

I handed over the practice test I had made the night before. Jessi put her head down and scribbled furiously. After ten minutes she slapped her pencil down. "Bam, all done," she said. "Go ahead, check my work!" she crowed, handing the papers to me.

I carefully checked them over. "Wow, Jessi, you aced it!"

She smiled and pumped a fist in the air. "I'm awesome!" she said, and laughed. "Actually, you are. You're the best tutor ever."

If Jessi could keep it up, she'd be a part of the Kicks again in time for our rematch against Pinewood!

After school I headed for the locker room to change for practice. None of us were expecting what was waiting for us on the field.

Coach Flores stood there, which was no surprise. But next to her was the coach of the boys' team, Coach Valentine. And on the field warming up were the boys!

"Seriously?" Zoe asked. She was still totally angry over how they'd called us losers at the dance. We all were.

"What, is their perfect field not good enough for them, they've got to play on our crummy one now too?" Grace sounded pretty mad. And I didn't blame her. The sight of Trey Bishop still made me want to punch him in the face, and he was there, warming up with the rest of them. I spotted Steven and Cody, too. What was going on?

Coach Valentine blew his whistle. "Gather round!" he barked.

We headed over, more than a little curious, yet eyeing the boys' team nervously as we huddled around the coaches.

"It has come to my attention that my boys have not been behaving with true sportsmanship off the field, which they know is required of them to be on my team," he shot them a stern look. The boys shuffled nervously and suddenly found something very interesting about their sneakers, because they all started staring at their feet.

Oops! I had forgotten that Coach Flores had gotten it out of me how the boys had teased us at the dance. So this is what this was about! I felt bad for Steven and Cody, who'd had nothing to do with it. But I know how team sports can be. If a few people mess up, the entire team can get punished.

"You are ALL Kangaroos," Coach Valentine went on, while Coach Flores nodded her approval as he spoke. "Not just the boys. Not just the girls. All of you. And you need to respect your other players always, no matter if they're having a good season or a bad season. So today we're all going to practice together to remind us that we're all in this together!"

Practice? With the boys? The girls' team began to groan, but Coach Valentine shot us a fierce look. "Ladies,

I'm not accepting complaints today, only hard work, so hit the field." He blew his whistle.

I exchanged wide-eyed glances with Emma. "Better do as he says," she whispered.

We ran onto the field with the boys' team. It was a weird feeling to be sharing the field with them.

First up the coaches had us practice passing, with the ball traveling through both teams. At first the teams stood apart, but Coach Flores put a stop to that. "Mix and mingle, people!" she said. I wouldn't have minded being near Steven, but the lucky thirteen on my practice T-shirt must have been on the fritz or something, because I ended up next to Trey. He didn't even look at me.

"Okeydokey, fellow Kangaroo," I whispered sarcastically under my breath. If he heard me, he didn't let on, just kept his eyes on the ball.

We kept doing drills. The boys' team was really good, and I could see why they were state champs last year. But we weren't the same team they had seen at the Pinewood game. We had improved a ton, and we held our own. The boys began to notice that.

"Devin, over here," Steven called when I got the ball. I lobbed a perfect pass to him.

Turns out Trey was actually paying attention. "Nice one," he admitted grudgingly.

Wow, something could come out of his mouth other than the word "loser." Impressive.

The coaches kept changing up the drills. We were split

into two teams and played a basic keep-away game. Good old thirteen must have finally warmed up, because I was on the same team as Steven.

"I'm sorry that some of these guys can be such jerks," he said to me as we got started.

"Me too," Cody said. He was also on our team.

"I'm just glad you're both not jerks too," I told them.

The game opened, with the other team trying to keep the ball away from my team.

Trey had control of the ball and needed to get rid of it because Steven was poised to pounce. I could see him looking for an open boy to pass it to, but there weren't any. "Zoe!" he called.

Zoe was ready. With Steven on him, Trey got off a less than clean kick. It went wide, and another player from the boys' team went for it. But Zoe zoomed in like a rocket, taking charge of the ball and moving it down the field before the other player had a chance to intercept. The other girls were equally impressive. Emma's newfound confidence as goalie had improved her skills out of the goal too. She targeted one of the boys, swooping in and stealing the ball before he could receive the pass. And she didn't trip once! We were holding our own and then some.

We kept playing for a while and then switched to some other drills before Coach Flores blew her whistle. Practice was over.

"Nice job!" she called. Coach Valentine smiled at us as we left the field. "Good hustle, girls," he said.

"That went better than I expected," Zoe said as we left the field. "And I think we proved to them that we're not losers!"

Now all we had to do was prove it to Mirabelle and the Panthers, too!

In homeroom the next morning an announcement was made over the loudspeaker that all of the Kicks needed to report to the gym during lunch. Now what?

When lunchtime finally came around, Jessi, Emma, and Zoe walked with me to the gym.

"Even though I'm not officially back on the Kicks yet, Coach Flores came around to my homeroom in person this morning to ask me to come too," Jessi said. She was so excited, she was bouncing on her toes as she walked. "She said she okayed it with my mom and everything!"

"I wonder what's going on," Emma said, her eyes shining. "I love surprises!"

When we got inside the gym with the other Kicks, we couldn't believe our eyes. The entire boys' soccer team was standing in the center of the room, along with Coach Valentine and Coach Flores. The smell of yummy, hot pizza wafted through the air. It was coming from a pile of unopened pizza boxes.

Cody and Trey Bishop came forward to greet us. Cody nudged Trey to start talking.

"So, I, um," Trey began. He looked over at Coach Valentine, who nodded encouragingly. "I wanted to apologize to you for how mean I was to you guys at the dance. I'm sorry I called you losers. You're not. You proved that yesterday. We were really impressed."

"Also," Cody jumped in, "we know you have a big rematch coming up against Pinewood."

"Yeah," said Trey. "So after practice yesterday, the guys and I decided that you deserved a pizza party, to help get you amped up for the big game," he said. "The Pinewood boys' team is our biggest rival too. Coach V. was right. We need to stick together as Kangaroos!" He sounded sincere.

"We also have a present for you," Cody said.

On cue Steven and another of the seventh-grade players came out of the boys' locker room holding a big banner. It had "Kentville Kicks" written across it in big letters.

"We were thinking we could help you decorate a banner for your pep rally tomorrow," Cody said. "Let's show those Panthers they can't *kick* around the Kangaroos!"

Wait, did Cody just say "*your* pep rally"? The Kicks all exchanged excited glances.

"No way," Emma said, and then cheered, clapping her hands together.

"We'll make sure the stands are packed for your game against the Pinewood Panthers too!" Steven added.

"Wow!" I couldn't believe it. I hugged Coach Flores. I knew she was behind all of this. It turns out, telling her what had happened at the dance was a good thing. A very good thing! I was so happy, I hugged Jessi, too. Even Coach Valentine. And all the Kicks. It was a huge hug fest as everyone joined in. I was so excited, I even grabbed Steven and gave him a big hug, but then I turned bright red. So did he!

Everyone began munching pizza and chattering happily as we decorated the banner together.

For the first time both the girls' and boys' Kangaroos felt like one big team. And I liked it.

The Kicks were all smiles as we gathered together in the hall behind the gymnasium the next day. We peeked through the doors as the auditorium filled up with our classmates.

"Can you believe they're all here for us?" Emma asked.

Grace smiled and shook her head. "This feels so good!"

"It's time! I'm going to go out there and introduce my girls," Coach Flores said proudly. "One of our captains should say a few words. Devin? Grace?"

Grace gave me a hug. "None of this would have happened if it weren't for Devin. Go for it!"

"Okay," I said, hugging her back. My stomach fluttered a little at the thought of talking in front of so many people. The butterflies had been on vacation, but looks like they were back! I glanced over at Zoe, who had her eyes tightly shut and was taking deep breaths. "You all right?" I asked.

"Yeah," she said. "I was starting to get nervous, so I'm using the techniques Frida taught me."

"She's doing great!" Frida beamed. "I think she should try out for the school play with me."

Zoe turned pale. "Soccer is one thing, but acting? I'll leave that to you!"

Coach Flores headed for the microphone set up at the front of the gym. "Students and staff of Kentville Middle School," she began. "Thank you for joining us today, on the day before our big rematch against the Pinewood Panthers girls' soccer team."

The audience booed. I guess we weren't the only ones who saw them as rivals.

"Now, please, put all your boos aside, and instead let's give a big round of applause for the Kentville Kangaroos girls' soccer team, or, as some of you know them, the Kicks!"

The auditorium cheered as our team, led by Emma, came ripping through the banner. My heart skipped a beat for a moment as Emma almost tripped and fell flat on her face. But she caught herself at the last minute and mimed a tip of the hat to the audience. The crowd loved it.

"And now a word from the Kangaroos' seventh-grade captain, Devin Burke!" Smiling, Coach Flores gave me a hug and handed me the microphone. "Good luck, kiddo," she whispered encouragingly.

The gym bleachers were filled with students, cheering and smiling at us. Some of them held signs that said GO, KANGAROOS. It seemed unreal. I couldn't believe I had come so far since that first scary day of school. And I couldn't believe how far the Kangaroos had come either! Suddenly I knew exactly what to say.

I took a deep breath. "I know we haven't been the

greatest team in the school so far this season, but we've been working really hard for this rematch against Pinewood. We hope you'll all come out to see how far we've come. The last time we played Pinewood, we lost. But this time we want to show them that we're not pushovers. I just found out that back in the nineties, the Kicks were state champs two years in a row. With your support, who knows where this season will take us. Come out on Saturday and cheer us on our way to a win!"

The boys' soccer team, sitting proudly in the front row, jumped to their feet, cheering. It was great to feel so supported, by them and by the entire school. It was almost like we were a completely different team from what we'd been just weeks ago. And it felt good. Now all we needed was for Jessi to do well on her test this afternoon. Once she rejoined the team, the Kicks would be complete!

"Ahhhhhhhhhhh!"

We were at practice later that day, running drills, when a shriek pierced the air.

Everyone stopped and turned to look. "I got an A!" Jessi cried, racing onto the practice field with her test paper in hand. "On my math test! Can you believe it? An A! My mom almost fainted!"

She skidded to a halt, panting.

"Oh my gosh, Jessi!" I cried. "You did it!"

The whole team gathered around her, excited to have her back.

"How'd you do it?" Frida asked.

"I couldn't have done it without Devin," she said, and she threw her arms around me.

We all squealed and jumped up and down together, excited that Jessi was back in time to join us for the big game. Now that we'd been working so hard to improve our skills, having Jessi back meant we would have a real chance against Pinewood.

"I know what life is like without soccer now." She shuddered. "Terrible!"

"We're so glad to have you back." Coach Flores beamed at her. "Isn't that right, girls?"

We all cheered in agreement.

Coach Flores blew her whistle. "Now let's get down to business and get ready to beat Pinewood!"

CHAPTER EIGHTEEN

When we got to the field for the big game Saturday afternoon, we couldn't believe our eyes. The stands were a sea of Kentville blue and white, packed with fans ready to cheer us on!

There were some Pinewood supporters there too, but the purple blotches were totally overwhelmed by Kentville blue. We actually had fans for a change. It felt awesome!

"Sock swap!" Grace called.

Our pregame ritual had become a team-wide tradition. Once Mirabelle had left, all the eighth graders had joined in on it too. We gathered in a circle, swapped socks with the person on our left, and put on the socks with our special toe wiggles, laughing and joking the entire time.

Before we headed onto the field for warm-ups, I said a few words to my team.

"Before she left, Mirabelle called us losers," I said. A bunch of the girls frowned, remembering how awful that had been. "Even though she was one of our best players, our team has grown stronger without her. In fact, it's a different team, a better team. So not only should we go out there today and prove that we're not losers, but let's show everyone we deserve to be called Kicks!" I cried.

Some of the girls started cheering and hooting.

Totally pumped, we raced onto the field for warm-ups. I touched my pink headband for luck before looking for my family in the stands. I spotted Dad, Mom, and Maisie. But there was a familiar face standing next to them, wearing a pink headband the same as mine.

"Kara!" I shrieked, racing over to hug her. I couldn't believe it! "What are you doing here?" She had on a very familiar shirt, my blue away jersey.

"My parents let me fly out to see you," she said, smiling from ear to ear. "It was so hard not to say anything when we talked on the phone!"

"Wow!" I began to tear up. I looked at my Mom and Dad. "How long have you been planning this?"

Dad gave me a wink. "Not too long," he said. "This all came together in the last couple of weeks."

I couldn't believe my luck. "Are you staying the whole weekend?" I asked.

"Of course!" she said. "It's our fall break, so I have a long weekend. I don't have to go back until Monday. You can give me the real California experience!"

I squealed and hugged her again. "I'm so glad you're here."

"You'd better get out there and finish warming up," Kara said. "I hope you and your Kicks kick some butt out there!" she said.

"We will!" I said. "Just for you!"

I turned to race back to my team.

"Wait!" my mom cried. She handed me a bottle of water. "Hydrate!"

I laughed. No matter how much things changed, some things would always stay the same.

With the game about to start, I had to turn my attention back to Pinewood. Across the field from us the Panthers were just breaking out of their pregame huddle. I spotted Mirabelle among the group. She looked over at me and sneered before holding her thumb and index finger up in the shape of an *L* and placing it on her forehead. Then she laughed.

I felt my cheeks turn bright red with anger. She was still calling us losers! A few of the other girls saw it and began muttering under their breath.

"Don't worry. We'll show her!" I said confidently. Mirabelle was going down!

Coach called us over. "Okay. You guys told me you didn't want to be pushed around by Pinewood again. Here's your chance to show them what the new and improved Kangaroos are made of. Got it?"

"Yeah!" we all cheered. I had never been more ready to

play, and before I knew it, the game was under way.

We had a shaky start. Pinewood was faster than we remembered, and they blitzed through our defense immediately. Each time, though, our new goalie, Emma, was right there, tipping the ball away from the goal.

"Our ball is black, our ball is white. Look out, Panthers, because we can fight!" she chanted.

I noticed a flaw on the field. "Defense, move up a bit! Don't let them push you out of the way," I tried to warn them, but the Panthers players were bigger and stronger. Number three's curved pass from the right corner was perfect, and one of the other Panthers slammed it home with her head. Even Emma couldn't stop that one. Score: 1–0, Panthers.

"Girls, we can't just rely on Emma in goal," Coach Flores yelled. "We have to be a team. Everyone needs to step it up." She was right.

On their next few attacks we managed to stuff the Panthers, with Frida charging around on defense. This game she was a vampire soccer player battling a team of werewolves. I know it sounds kooky, but we wanted her to be as aggressive as possible for our rematch against Pinewood. And it was working! She was playing just as assertively as the Pinewood forwards. I just hoped she didn't get so into character that she tried to bite anyone!

"Watch out, you bunch of furballs!" she yelled.

The Panthers eyed her nervously and kept their distance. She sounded crazy!

Our defenders couldn't seem to control Mirabelle. She consistently broke free and dribbled her way through our defense, sneering and laughing at us as she did. With her putting on that kind of pressure, it was only a matter of time before she put the ball in the net. Emma lunged at Mirabelle's next shot but missed. Now we were down two goals.

"Losers!" Mirabelle yelled after her goal.

Jessi's eyes narrowed, and I thought she was going to land a flying tackle on Mirabelle.

"Shake it off," I told her. "She wants to get under our skin. Don't let her do it!"

Jessi exhaled loudly. "You're right," she said, and her face brightened. "Maybe I'll get under her skin instead!"

But Mirabelle and the rest of the Panthers were getting to the rest of the Kicks. I began to get worried. It seemed like we were trying our best, almost more than our best, but it wasn't working. We were still at 2–0, Panthers. It wasn't even halftime yet and our team was playing so hard that we were becoming exhausted.

Coach Flores then changed everything by calling in an adjustment.

"Jessi, cover Mirabelle!" she said.

Jessi got an evil smile on her face. "My pleasure," she said. Good thing Jessi wasn't the one pretending to be a vampire!

Coach's move was brilliant! Even though Jessi wasn't normally a defender, she was just as athletic as Mirabelle.

She shadowed Mirabelle all around the field, getting in the way of any pass headed her way.

"Jessi, get away from me!" Mirabelle hissed. But Jessi wasn't doing anything wrong, just covering Mirabelle perfectly. After a few tries the other Panthers stopped trying to feed Mirabelle the ball.

Mirabelle got so angry, she whirled toward Jessi and shoved her hard. Jessi hit the ground, and the ref whistled Mirabelle for a yellow card.

"One more like that, and you're out of here," he said.

"Come on, Mirabelle. Push me again," Jessi taunted.

Still furious, Mirabelle actually grew flustered and ran haphazardly around the field, trying to do anything to get Jessi off her. I'd never seen Mirabelle so uncomfortable before.

"What's the matter, Mirabelle, you can't shake this loser?" Jessi was totally enjoying herself.

"I can't believe I was ever friends with someone like you." Mirabelle practically spit the words out, she was so mad.

Jessi just grinned at her. "That makes two of us," she said.

When halftime came, the Kentville Kangaroos were still down 2–0. After the Panthers' initial blitz we'd basically played them to a standstill. We still had a chance!

"Remember, if we lose this game, we're all still winners," Coach said. "You guys are already doing so great out there."

"We want to be *actual* winners this time, Coach Flores," I insisted. It was great that we were playing better than we ever had before, but we wanted this win. "We've come this far, and we've proven that we can hang with them. I know our defensive strategy got us here, but we need to be able to score, too. What do you think, Coach, can we push and try to get a few goals?"

"If we do that, we risk losing control of the game," Coach said. But then she got a mischievous gleam in her eyes. "But if you're willing to risk it, so am I."

She worked on a new game plan, one that was riskier but with more reward if we could pull it off.

I knew we had a chance. Pinewood wasn't used to teams standing up to them. Not only was Mirabelle frustrated, their entire team was. They wouldn't know how to react if we turned the tables on them.

We needed an X factor, though—or in this case a Z factor. Zoe!

I knew that Zoe needed to be the star of the second half for us to win. With Jessi blanketing Mirabelle, Zoe was the only person who could lead us to victory.

Before we got back on the field, I pulled her aside.

"Zoe, this is it. You have to be the star right now. Jessi's stuck on Mirabelle, and the rest of us are holding off the Panthers offense, but we need to score. You can do it."

Zoe nodded, taking in what I had to say. She took a deep breath. "Got it." She smiled. Thanks to Frida, Zoe was now a confident kick-butt player!

"I'm going to get you the ball, and we're gonna bring the game to them, okay?" I said.

When the second half started, Pinewood turned up their aggressiveness another notch too. I hadn't counted on that. With our defense still smothering them, the Panthers started to panic, and they pushed and shoved on every possession. The referees were not helping us out.

Coach hollered from the sidelines, "Pay attention, ref! Look at what they're doing!"

"You mangy mutts!" Frida hollered, baring her teeth. Despite their rough tactics, Zoe managed to find a seam in Pinewood's defense and zipped through for a break-away goal. The crowd went wild. We were now 2–1!

Zoe was able to squeeze through the Pinewood defense again, and on the next trip down the field, she had another clear path to the goal, until a Pinewood defender slid in and tripped her.

Zoe lay flat on the ground. Shockingly, there was no whistle from the referee. The crowd began to boo.

We ran over to pick Zoe up, but she bounced right up off the grass, ready to go once again. Once Zoe was unleashed, she was unstoppable. Using her quickness, she raced from sideline to sideline, completely disrupting the Pinewood defense.

Her offense helped our defense, since all the attention Pinewood paid her took away from their own game. The Panthers coach even subbed in another defender, because Zoe couldn't be stopped. When Zoe scored again despite the extra attention, we had a 2–2 tie. Our fans roared their approval.

On the sideline Coach Flores screamed encouragements at us, even as she yelled at the referees to pay attention to the rough play from the Panthers' side. Finally the referee gave the entire Panthers team a warning.

That made Zoe even harder to corral. When I lobbed her a pass and she scored again a few minutes later, from an impossible angle, our crowd erupted and started cheering harder.

With Mirabelle completely neutralized by Jessi, we now had the upper hand. Zoe scored another goal for a hat trick, and Pinewood collapsed. Mirabelle started arguing with some of the other Panthers, frustrated after falling behind. They stopped working together.

With a few minutes left in the game, the score was 3–2 Kangaroos. The momentum was fully on our side. The win was so close, we could feel it. But I had one more thing on my mind: payback. I ran over to Jessi and whispered to her that I wanted to take on Mirabelle. At first she looked confused, but then she grinned.

"You got it. I'll set you up." She knew exactly what I had in mind.

Game time was winding down. Jessi passed the ball to me, setting me up for a one on one versus Mirabelle. I knew Mirabelle was so angry, she wouldn't back down, even if the rest of her team had given up.

Mirabelle had been a bully of a captain. She'd laughed

at her own teammates and called them losers. It was time to show her how wrong she was.

With a fake-out move that Coach had taught me, I zoomed right past Mirabelle. Her eyes grew wide and her mouth opened in surprise, before her face crumbled in disappointment as she realized what was happening. Leaving her in the dust, I punched the ball past the Panthers' goalie. Goal! The final whistle sounded.

We had done it! The Kentville Kangaroos had beaten the Pinewood Panthers! Our fans went wild.

Mirabelle looked at me, her mouth open.

"We're not losers, Mirabelle," I said, smiling. "And we never were!"

She stamped her feet before storming off the field. But I had better things to do than watch her pout. The Kangaroos and Coach Flores came running over together, hugging one another and screaming in happiness.

"We did it!" Emma yelled, jumping up and down with excitement.

"Awesome game!" I told everyone. Nothing could wipe this smile off my face, but something happened to make it even bigger.

Our fans flooded the field, led by the boys' team. They chanted, "Kicks, Kicks," while my teammates gleefully lifted me up on their shoulders. This was even better than the dream I'd had the day school had started!

"Nice job, Devin!" a boy's voice called up to me. I looked down to see Steven there, grinning.

I smiled. "Thanks!"

After the girls put me down, I took a moment to soak it all in. I watched as the boys' team congratulated my teammates, smiling and slapping them on the backs. Emma was circled by her huge family, and they were all chanting her name as she took a bow in the middle. Mr. and Mrs. Dukes were all smiles as they hugged Jessi. People were lining up to shake Zoe's hand; she had been a true star. Frida came out of character to share a group hug with Brianna, Sarah, and Anna. Grace, Anjali, and several of the other eighth graders were laughing as they splashed a beaming Coach Flores with Gatorade.

And best of all, my mom, dad, Maisie, and Kara came rushing over to hug me. "Devin, we're so proud of you," my mom said as my dad ruffled my hair.

"Way to go!" Maisie cheered, while Kara grabbed my hand.

"So I guess California isn't so bad after all, is it?" Kara teased with a grin.

No, and with the Kicks by my side, I couldn't wait to find out what else California had in store for me!

GLOSSARY

corner kick: If a defender kicks the ball out of bounds over the goal line, a member of the attacking team gets a free kick from the nearest corner of the field.

defender: The defenders on a soccer team are the players who line up in front of their team's goal and try to keep the ball away from the goal. Defenders can also move the ball offensively across the field.

double tap: When dribbling, a player gives the ball two short, quick taps in a row.

dribble: When a player dribbles the ball, she runs while kicking the ball at the same time, trying to keep possession and control of the ball.

drill: A training exercise.

flanks: A player on the flank of the field has a position on either the far left or far right side.

forward: Also known as strikers, forwards are the team's main attackers and spend most of the game in the opponent's half of the field.

goalie: Also known as the goalkeeper. The goalie's job is to defend the goal. She is the only player on the team who can use her hands.

hat trick: A hat trick is when a player scores three goals in one game. A flawless hat trick is when a player scores three goals in a row in the same game.

interception: When a player gains control of the ball by taking possession of it from the opposing team.

juggling: A player juggles a soccer ball in the air by repeatedly bouncing the ball off her feet.

left wing: Any offensive player who plays on the left side of the field.

mercy rule: This rule allows the refs to end a soccer game early when one team has what looks like an unbeatable lead over the other team.

midfielder: The midfielders play in front of the defenders and behind the forwards. They generally have to be well-rounded players, good at both defending and scoring goals.

offsides: An offensive player is offsides if she does not have possession of the ball and there is no defender between her and the opposing team's goal.

one-time: When a player shoots the ball directly from a pass.

pass: When a player kicks the ball to another player on the same team.

red card: A red card is shown to a player by the referee for serious misconduct on the field. The player is ejected from the game immediately and cannot return.

scrimmage: Also known as "friendlies," these are practice games that follow the regular rules of soccer but do not count toward team statistics or wins.

step-over: A move made by a player dribbling the ball to fool the defensive player into thinking she is going to move in a different direction.

striker: Also known as forwards, strikers are the team's main attackers and spend most of the game in the opponent's half of the field.

yellow card: The referee shows the yellow card to a player as a warning that she is breaking the rules of the game, usually by displaying unsporting behavior. If a player gets two yellow cards in the same game, she can no longer play in that game.

A NOTE FROM ALEX

Hey guys,

Thank you so much for reading *Saving the Team*! I hope you had as much fun reading it as I had writing it.

If you were wondering why a soccer player would want to write a book series like the Kicks, the answer is easy. When I was a kid, books were almost as important to me as soccer. My favorites were *Matilda* by Roald Dahl and *Ella Enchanted* by Gail Carson Levine—stories about girls going after their dreams, even in the face of adversity and unlikely odds. They inspired me to be dedicated, and I hope reading about Devin and her challenges will inspire you, too.

In sports and in life, there are so many chances to fail. It's easy to give up sometimes. But as long as you keep dreaming and stay true to what you want in life, the impossible suddenly becomes possible.

I credit *so* much of my success to commitment. I've been committed to being a professional soccer player since I was eight years old, when I wrote this note on a Post-it:

My mom put that note on the fridge and, as silly as it may sound, having that note up there strengthened my resolve. I was committed to making my dream a reality. Just like Devin is committed to being co-captain and making the Kangaroos the best team they can be.

It helps being surrounded by great people too. My family is always there for me. My dad has never missed a National Team game! And the US Women's National Soccer Team is my second family. We work together, travel together, and even live together. If we didn't get along so well, both off the field and on, we wouldn't be a gold-medal-winning team. Likewise, without Jessi, Emma, and Zoe, Devin never would have worked so hard to help make the team great.

Finally, I'm so lucky to have *you* cheering me on! Writing this book series for you is my way of returning the favor. I hope you liked *Saving the Team* and you'll pick up the next book in the series, *Sabotage Season*. In the meantime, if you have any questions you'd like answered, feel free to write me at @alexmorgan13 on Twitter or at facebook.com/AlexMorganSoccer.

Oh, and one last thing: Just because I knew what I wanted to be when I was eight, don't feel like you have to know now what you're going to do when you grow up. There are lots of ways to get where you're going. Just follow your passion and be true to yourself.

See you soon,
Alex

want more of
alex morgan's the kicks?
here's a sneak peak at
book two in the series,
available now!

"Devin? Is that you?"

I set down the huge bag of soccer balls I was carrying and turned to see Coach Flores behind me.

"Hi, Coach," I said. "I thought I'd set up the practice field early, since it's my turn to run practice today."

Coach smiled at me. "Need any help? I was just doing some paperwork in my office when I heard noise in the equipment room, but I can finish up later if you want."

I shook my head. "Thanks, but there's not much to do. I kind of want to get my head ready too. Know what I mean?"

She nodded. "Back in the day, my mom used to bring me to the field an hour before we had to report for each game, but I didn't mind. It helped me to calm down and focus."

"Exactly," I agreed.

Coach headed back to her office, and I carried the balls from the equipment room out to the Kentville Middle School soccer field. I had to admit, I was feeling pretty pumped up. First, the boys' team was at an away game, so we got to use their practice field instead of our crummy field of weeds with garbage cans for goalposts. Second, Coach had said that the team co-captains could each run a practice this week to get leadership experience, and today was my turn. And the third reason was that I had figured out something awesome.

Our team, the Kentville Kangaroos (otherwise known as the Kicks), had a shot at making the play-offs! When I first joined the team, I never thought we had a chance. At the start of the season, we were pretty awful. We lost a bunch of games, but then we figured things out, and we got a lot better. We tied a game, and we even beat the Pinewood Panthers—a really strong team—the second time we played them. And now there was actually a chance—a small one—that we could make the play-offs. I knew if we worked hard, we could keep winning, and that made me happy. As co-captain, it was part of my job to make sure we were the best team we could be.

The afternoon sun shone down on the field, and I admired the perfectly trimmed green grass and the freshly painted white lines. I dumped out the balls and then started dribbling around the circumference of the field, just because I could.

"Hey, Devin! Don't tire yourself out!"

I squinted and saw my friend Jessi walking onto the field. She was the first person I'd made friends with when I'd moved to Kentville a few months before, and in addition to my friend Kara back in Connecticut, Jessi was one of my best friends.

I dribbled up to her. "You're here just in time to help me set up the cones," I said.

She grinned. "Anything for my captain."

"Co-captain," I reminded her. "Anyway, I'm psyched for practice. I stayed up last night looking at some drills online. I've got some new stuff we can try out."

"I don't know. I kind of liked Grace's last practice," Jessi said, mentioning the eighth grader who co-captained the team with me. "Some dribbling, a scrimmage, and then done. Not too stressful."

"Well, I've got some defensive drills for us," I told her. "I know we beat the Panthers last time, but they had way too many scoring attempts in that game. I found a couple of drills that I think are really going to make our blocking and intercepting skills better."

"Whoa, you're totally taking this seriously," Jessi said.

"Well, I found something out," I said. "After we beat the Panthers, I checked the stats in our division. The Panthers and the Vipers are pretty much guaranteed play-off spots. But the third and fourth places are open. If we keep winning, we could get one of those slots."

Jessi raised an eyebrow. "Seriously? The Kicks? In the play-offs?"

I nodded. "It could happen."

Jessi grinned. "Then bring it on!"

"I will," I promised. "Come on. Let's go get those cones."

We set up the cones to form two squares on the field for the first drill I had in mind. A few minutes later the other players started showing up. Emma and Zoe walked over to me and Jessi as we finished setting up. The two of them were good friends but they were also pretty opposite. Emma was tall and tan and athletic, and she could be a total klutz on the field unless she was in goal. Zoe was petite with short strawberry-blond hair, and she was super-agile and sure on her feet. She'd been playing forward a lot recently because she had this way of zigzagging through the other team's defenders and getting right to the goal.

"Yay! It's Devin's practice day!" Emma cheered.

"I found some new drills we can try," I said.

"Devin says we can make the play-offs if we keep winning games," Jessi reported.

Zoe cocked her head. "Us? Really?"

I laughed. "Why does everyone keep saying that? It's not impossible."

Jessi patted me on the back. "Well, we can dream."

"To dream the impossible dream!"

We all turned at the sound of someone singing in an operatic voice. It was Frida, of course. Besides playing soccer, she was a total drama nut.

"Bravo! Bravo!" Emma cried, clapping.

"Actually, it's '*brava*' when it's a girl," Frida corrected. "But thank you." She took a little bow.

Coach Flores blew the whistle, which meant it was time for practice to start. We ran to join the rest of the Kicks, and I was surprised to notice that it seemed not all the girls were there. I did a quick count—there were twelve of us, but there should have been nineteen.

"Where is everybody?" I asked.

Coach shrugged. "They must be running late. But go ahead and start, Devin."

I nodded. "Okay. Let's do some stretches to warm up."

I led everyone in stretches, and then we ran around the field once to get our hearts pumping. As I ran, I made a mental list of everyone who was missing—three seventh graders and four eighth graders, including Grace. It was kind of weird.

The missing players still hadn't showed up when we were done running, so I went ahead and started the first drill.

"Okay!" I told everyone. "So this first drill is a variation on Monkey in the Middle. There are a few ways to do it, but we're going to focus on our intercepting skills."

I counted down the line of players, "One, two, one, two," until everyone had a number. "Okay, ones, please form a circle inside that square we've marked out with cones. Twos, form a circle inside the other square."

My teammates formed the circles quickly, and then I pulled out two girls from each circle to stand in the middle—Brianna and Taylor in one circle, and Frida and Jade in the other.

"Okay. Here's how this works," I said. "Girls on the outside, you're playing offense. Your goal is to keep passing the ball to one another for as long as you can. Girls on the inside, you're defense. Your goal is to intercept or block the passes between the offensive players. If you succeed, the offensive player who made the pass has to switch places with you."

I threw a ball to each circle. "Ready, go!"

Emma made the first kick in her circle, and it flew right over Brianna's head.

"Whoops!" Emma cried.

"Got it!" Maya, an eighth grader who usually played midfielder, stopped the ball with her knee and sent it skidding across the circle, low but fast. This time Brianna stopped the ball with her foot. Then she and Maya switched places.

Both circles got the hang of it really quickly, and Coach Flores helped me out by giving pointers to the girls trying to defend. After a few minutes you could start to see what everyone's strengths and weaknesses were. Jade, an eighth grade defender, easily intercepted the first pass that came at her. Zoe, who was a strong offensive player when she was dribbling, was having trouble passing to players across the circle. She just didn't have enough power behind her kicks. And Frida was stuck in the middle for a long time. She couldn't get where she needed to be in time. But I knew that everyone was trying their hardest.

"Great job!" I called after we had played for about twenty minutes. "Let's clear the cones."

"Hey, there's Grace!" Brianna called out.

I turned and saw Grace and the rest of the missing girls walking onto the field. They looked puzzled to see us practicing.

I jogged up to Grace.

"Did you guys start already?" she asked.

I nodded. "Yeah, about a half hour ago."

She frowned. "But Coach Flores e-mailed that practice was starting late today."

Coach Flores had overheard. "I didn't do that. Are you sure it was from me?"

Grace and the other girls nodded.

"It came from your e-mail address," said Sarah.

Coach shook her head. "That is so strange. Maybe it was an old e-mail that you saw? That happens sometimes. An old e-mail pops up out of nowhere."

"Like it was stuck in limbo or something," Emma added.

"Well, sorry you guys missed the first drill, but we're about to do another one," I said. "Do you want to warm up first?"

"Just give us a minute to stretch," Grace replied.

I was feeling a little impatient, but I didn't show it. "We might as well all stretch!"

After a few more minutes of stretching, I clapped my hands, eager to start the next drill.

"It's time for a shoot-out! Emma, take the goal!"

Emma was kind of all over the place when she was on the field, but I'd discovered that she made an excellent goalie. She jogged over to the goal, and I got the other players to line up in two lines, with the first person in line facing the goal—one line on the right, and one line on the left.

"This one is fast and furious," I said. "Emma will start out as goalie. First player on the right will take a shot at the goal and then run to the back of the line. Then a player on the left will take a shot. Keep going until everyone has a turn, and then we'll switch goalies."

Giselle, an eighth grader with curly blond hair, looked at me with wide eyes. "You mean we *all* have to take the goal?"

"On a well-rounded team, everybody needs to know how to play every position," I told her. I knew that sounded kind of preachy, but I had done a lot of reading about coaching over the past few days to prep for this, and that idea had come up a lot. Giselle didn't look too happy, but I wasn't going to change the practice. We had to make sure we had a good backup goalie in case Emma couldn't play in a game.

"Ready, go!" I yelled once we were set up. Jessi ran up to make the first kick.

Wham! She sent the ball flying high and fast, and Emma had to jump up to block it. She slammed it down just as the next ball came whizzing past her feet.

Emma proved what a great goalie she was, because the pace was intense and she blocked more balls than she let get past her. When we came to the end of the line, I sent Jessi into the goal. She got into it with more energy than I had ever seen, diving and jumping.

Just like with the first drill, it became pretty clear what the players' strengths were, and who had goal-keeping in their blood. Sarah, a seventh grader, was really fast and kept her eye on the ball. And Zarine, who was in eighth grade and usually played midfield, made this amazing save where she jumped sideways to catch the ball in midair and then landed by somersaulting on the grass.

"Your turn, Devin!" Jessi called out when the last girl had taken her turn.

"Oh, yeah. Of course!" I replied, running to take my place. Just because I was running the practice didn't mean I couldn't participate in the drill.

I slipped on the goalie gloves and got ready for the onslaught. I didn't have to wait long.

Wham! Brianna sent a ball sailing past my head.

"I wasn't ready!" I protested.

"A goalie always needs to be ready!" Emma yelled back, laughing, and I knew she was right. I narrowed my eyes and waited for the next ball. Grace kicked it, and it came speeding across the grass, low and fast, aimed for the lower right corner of the goal. I dove for it, skidded across the grass, and blocked it just in time.

No sooner was I back on my feet than Sarah launched the next ball into the air, and I raced across the goal to stop it.

Wow, this is a pretty tough drill, I realized, but I didn't let on. I gave every shot my best, and managed to block about half of them. After the last shot blew past me, I jogged up to Emma.

"Have I told you lately what an awesome goalie you are?" I asked, breathing hard. "That is hard work."

Emma grinned. "Yeah, but I love it," she said. "Although, some nights I dream that soccer balls are flying past my head—like, thousands of them—and I can't stop them."

I nodded. "I can see why," I said, and then I turned to the rest of the team. "Okay, let's scrimmage! I'll count off teams."

We had all nineteen girls now, including me, so I put nine people on a team and I coached from the sideline. Since Zarine had done so well in the last drill, I put her in goal for her team. She seemed a little nervous at first, but I could see her get more comfortable with it as the scrimmage went on.

It seemed like only a few minutes had passed when Coach Flores tapped me on the shoulder.

"Devin, we should end the game," she said. "Great practice."

"Already?" I asked. "I was hoping to do one more quick drill at the end."

Coach nodded toward the parking lot, where some parents were already waiting in cars. "We're running a little late already. Sorry."

"More drills? You really are a *drill* sergeant," Jessi teased. "I, for one, am ready for a shower and some dinner."

"Admit it. It was fun," I said.

Frida walked up to us, her hands on her hips. "Fun and exhausting," she said.

After we put the equipment away, Jessi, Emma, Zoe, Frida, and I walked toward the parking lot.

"Hey, I wanted to tell you guys," Frida said. "So, you know how my mom made me play soccer? Well, she's so happy that I am putting my 'best effort' into it, as she says, that she signed me up for a weekly acting class. Isn't that great? I start tomorrow."

"That sounds perfect for you," Emma agreed.

"It's a win-win," Frida said. "I ended up liking soccer, and now I get to keep acting, too."

I wasn't so sure. "You start tomorrow? Couldn't it wait until after soccer season? What if it interferes with your practice?"

"Relax, Devin," Frida said. "It's only one day a week, when we don't have practice."

"In Devin's perfect world every day would be a practice day," Jessi teased. "Practice after breakfast, practice during lunch break . . ."

"Midnight practice," Emma joined in. "And sunrise practice."

"Okay, okay, I get it," I said, laughing. "I'm happy for you, Frida. Seriously."

"Be happy for me once my mom lets me start auditioning again," Frida said. "Shawna Young from my old acting class just got a part on a TV show, and I *know* I'm a better actor than she is."

Just then my mom's car pulled up, so I waved to my friends. "Got to go. See you tomorrow."

I ran to the car, and when I opened the door, really loud pop music blared out. In the backseat my sister Maisie was bopping up and down.

"Seriously, does it have to be this loud?" I asked.

"Yes, it does!" Maisie yelled from the back.

Mom turned the sound down a little bit. "How did practice go?" she asked.

"Great," I replied. "I didn't get to do all the drills I wanted, but the ones we did were really good."

"Of course they were," Mom said. "That's my dedicated Devin."

"Turn it up!" Maisie yelled.

Everyone said that Maisie and I looked alike, and I guessed we did, because we both had brown eyes and straight brown hair, although Maisie's was shorter than mine. But just because we looked alike didn't mean we *were* alike. I was a pretty chill person (well, except on the soccer field), and Maisie was like an eight-year-old tornado.

"Maisie, please use your car voice," Mom scolded, and I quickly dug my earbuds out of my duffel bag and turned on my own music so I could make it home without going crazy.

Once we got home, I quickly showered and then turned on my laptop in my bedroom. After Kara's last visit we'd decided to do a webcam chat once a day if we could, so we could see each other's faces. But sometimes it was hard to find the right time because it was always three hours later in Connecticut.

"Devin!" Kara cried happily when her face popped up on my screen. The webcam was amazing because I could see every freckle on Kara's face.

"Hey!" I said. "What's up?"

"Still dreaming about my weekend in California with you," she answered. "It's amazing there! It's so sunny and beautiful. And I still can't believe that we actually went to Hollywood. And how close you are to Disneyland! It must be like being on vacation all the time."

"It kind of felt like that at first," I admitted. "But now it's like, you know, life. Like, tonight I have a ton of homework."

"I did too," Kara said, making a face. "But I just finished. High-five!"

She held her palm up in front of the camera, and I did the same. Kara cracked me up sometimes.

"Oh, hey," I said. "I have been dying to tell you something all day. I just figured out that the Kicks might have a chance at the play-offs—if we focus. Can you believe that? After those losses we had in the beginning."

"That's awesome," Kara said. "Focusing is good. Although, I don't know how you can focus with that guy Steven staring at you the whole time."

I blushed. "What?" I asked, but I knew what she meant.

"Steven, that guy with the spiky hair," Kara replied. "When I saw you in that game against the Panthers, he sat near us, and I swear he was staring at you the whole entire game."

"He was not," I protested.

"He's cute!" Kara said. "I wish somebody that cute would stare at me."

"Fine, he's cute," I admitted. "But I can't think about stuff like that right now. I need to focus on school and on the Kicks until the season is over."

"Maybe Steven is thinking about you right now," Kara teased. "Devin and Steven. It kind of rhymes."

Then she began to sing, "Devin and Steven. Devin and Steven—"

"No distractions!" I yelled, and then we both collapsed into giggles.

Every time I talked to Kara, I realized how much I missed her. The webcam was nice, but it was just not the same as being with her in person. Sometimes I daydreamed that Kara and her family moved out to California and she joined the Kicks. If that could have happened, I thought my life would have been pretty perfect!